WITCH IN DISGUISE

A BLAIR WILKES MYSTERY

ELLE ADAMS

"Miaow." Sky the cat swatted me awake, digging his claw into my cheek just hard enough to make me sit up. "Miaow."

"Miaow yourself," I said thickly. My throat was clogged up, my eyes were dry and burning, and my head pounded. Why did I feel like the living dead? Oh, right. It was my first day back at work since my life had imploded.

Past Blair had helpfully left a to-do list on the bedside table. It read:

Go to work.

Act normal.

Find out location of the paranormal prison my father is locked away in.

Bonus: find out why Nathan locked him up in the first place.

It all seemed a little too much for a Monday.

Go to work… no problem. Act normal… might be difficult. Paranormal prison… I'd deal with that one later.

As for Nathan, I'd be best off not seeing him at all until

I got my head—and life—back together.

First, I went to the bathroom, grimacing at my reflection in the mirror. Angry red splotches on my face, tangled dark brown hair, zombified expression. Maybe normal was some way off. A flash of glitter caught my eye and for a moment I half expected to see another face replace mine, with glittering skin and pointed ears, but the only glitter in here was Alissa's luminescent shower gel. *You're losing it, Blair.*

After I'd showered and dressed, drying my hair with a wave of my wand—and silently thanking Alissa for teaching me that spell—I returned to my room to find a pixie fluttering above my bed. The small flitting creature had been randomly appearing in the flat for weeks, and generally, only I could see it. It was about eight inches tall, with little pointed ears jutting from behind tufts of thick blond hair, and was clothed in a bark-coloured shirt and trousers. It was also covered in glitter. Maybe I wasn't cracking up after all.

The pixie landed on the scrap of paper I'd left out on my bedside table. I'd spent the last few days writing and rewriting a response to the note left by my father, who was currently locked in a secure paranormal prison. His note hadn't said *why* he'd been locked up, only that he'd wanted to meet me. Thanks to a wizard murderer and his nasty monster pet hiding in the forest, I'd missed that meeting and wouldn't get another one until the next solstice. It was barely July, and I had a long summer ahead.

"Sure," I said to the pixie. "Go ahead, take it to him."

The pixie picked up the note, then vanished in a swirl of glitter. Thanks to that little creature, I was constantly picking glitter out of my clothes and hair. It seemed to shed everywhere. Maybe a fairy thing. I was far from an expert despite *being* half fairy, partly because I'd never met the fairy side of my birth family. In the note, I'd ended up just giving my dad a brief summary of my life, and adding that I'd like to see him if they ever let him out of the jail again. I hadn't quite had the courage to ask what he'd done to get locked up—I'd ask him later, or if we ever got to speak face to face.

I had too many questions to put in a simple letter. I'd barely been a year old when I'd been put into foster care and as far as I'd known since then, I'd been normal. I'd kept the note brief in the end, not wanting to get into my history of losing jobs and drifting around and never fitting in anywhere. Fairy Falls was the closest I'd felt to home, and I'd even messed that up when I'd neglected to tell the guy I was sort-of-seeing that I was half fairy and then de-glamoured in front of half the town.

"You look like you just slept in a coffin," said Alissa, my flatmate, sipping coffee at the kitchen table when I walked in. Her cat, Roald, lay curled around her feet, occasionally swatting at Sky when he got too close. Sprawled under the table, Sky looked non-threatening, a little black cat with one white paw, and one grey and one blue eye—but his other form was a terrifying beast.

When I'd adopted Sky—or rather, he'd adopted me—everyone had assumed he was a witch's familiar and had picked me for that reason. Instead, he'd turned out to be a fairy cat who could shapeshift, walk through walls, and pick up on the psychic projections of vampires. Oh, and turn into a giant furry monster. And I wondered why I could never get used to this new 'normal'.

"Most vampires look more alert than I do," I said, walking to the kitchen counter. "Apparently, immortality means being able to sleep in coffins without waking up with horrible back pain."

"Most vampires line their coffins with cushions," she said. "Not that it sounds fun either way. What if you forget about the coffin lid and hit your head in the middle of the night?"

"Exactly." Since Alissa had been sort-of-dating a vampire until recently, she'd know all about the downsides. "That's why I'd make a terrible vampire. Not that I'm a great fairy either..." I clamped my mouth shut before I started listing all my woes. *Act normal, remember?*

Alissa gave me a concerned look as I brought my mug of the caffeinated witchy brew to the table. "Are you okay, Blair?"

"What did my fairy form actually look like?" I blurted. "It's not like there were any mirrors around when we were running for our lives."

She blinked. "Winged. Shiny. Otherwise, basically like you. Why?"

I shook my head. "The way everyone stared, it was like I'd turned into an elf or something."

"Oh, no," she said. "The elves are barely related to you. Really, don't worry about it. Everyone will have forgotten soon."

I sincerely doubted they'd forgotten my public performance that easily. "I hope it's a calm day at the office." I'd been allowed a few days off to recover from my latest ordeal—in this case, being the prisoner of a mad wizard in his ancestor's house—but at least my co-workers already knew I was half fairy. That would make things easier. And let's face it, they'd seen me screw up before. I'd once accidentally turned myself transparent for two full days when I'd tried to make an invisibility potion.

"Do you have a magic lesson later?" Alissa asked.

I took a long sip of coffee. "Yep. I'm going to beg Rita to keep me in individual classes for now, but to start at a higher level. Mostly so I stop accidentally creating spontaneous glitter balls."

Let's just say I'd had a little trouble learning to use my wand, at least until I'd figured out that I was actually left-wand-handed and not right-handed like I was with everything else. Even then, my magic was erratic, reacted in response to emotions without conscious thought, and generally didn't behave in the way it was supposed to.

She snorted. "You're not wrong. If it's any consolation, you have a ton of raw talent, but you just haven't learned to control it in the right way."

"Is Madame Grey going to be there?" I asked. "I know she's still busy dealing with complaints from the werewolves and the vampires, but I wanted to talk to her."

"If she has any sense, she's run off," Alissa said. "They won't give her a moment's peace. What, did you want to talk about your magical training with her, or...?"

I sipped my coffee, twisting my hands around the mug. "Yeah... and no. I just sent a message with the pixie, but I can't help wondering if she knows the number for the Lancashire Prison for Paranormals so I can contact my dad."

Alissa's expression filled with pity, which I'd expected. "Maybe, but... they don't allow visits. As far as I know, anyway. I'm sorry."

I nodded, disappointment seeping through me. It

sounded like the paranormal prison made Fairy Falls's gargoyle law enforcement look like cuddly bunnies. And if it turned out my father had committed a horrible crime, then maybe it was for the best that he stayed behind bars. And yet... I wanted to know the truth. Of course, since Nathan had arrested my father, it was possible *he* knew— but the idea of facing him seemed as appealing as spending the night in a coffin.

I'd considered sending Sky to pay the prison a visit, since he could walk through walls, but I needed to find out where the prison actually *was*. The pixie had gone to deliver the letter, so I'd see if my dad sent a response and then decide what to do.

I put my coffee mug aside. "Right. Best get to work."

"Good luck," Alissa told me as I gathered my things.

I needed more than luck to avoid the endless stares. I'd hoped to gradually break the news that I was half fairy, not expose myself in a public display. Steeling myself, I walked outside.

Most people travelled on foot in Fairy Falls, since it was a small town and magic caused most human technology to malfunction, so the streets were packed with people walking to work. I figured flying to work using my Seven Millimetre Boots would attract too much attention, but everyone stared anyway. I put my head down, walking as quickly as I could. Did they expect me to talk to them? Maybe tell a joke? Or de-glamour and fly around like I'd done when the disguise had come off?

The 'act normal' part of my plan wasn't going well, and a flood of relief hit me when I reached the office of Dritch & Co, my employers. Okay, maybe striving for normal when I worked for a paranormal recruitment firm was an impossibility, but my co-workers were friendly and my boss seemed to like me, too.

Callie, the receptionist, glanced up as I walked in. The blond werewolf harboured no hard feelings towards me for the latest catastrophe—which was more than I could say for her family—but she didn't give me her usual friendly wave. I gritted my teeth and entered the half open door to the main office.

Two of my fellow co-workers were already there. To my relief, Lizzie and Bethan both waved at me. The latter was the daughter of the boss, a woman of around my age with straight dark hair and pale skin, whose magical gift allowed her to do the work of five people at once. And then there was Lizzie—dark-skinned with delicate features, and creator of the office's heavenly coffee machine. Her speciality was magical technology. The newest member, Lena, wasn't here yet.

"The boss is acting weird," said Bethan. "Fair warning. Otherwise, today's list is pretty light. I asked her to go easy on you."

"Thanks," I said gratefully. "I appreciate it."

I busied myself organising my desk to avoid their stares, knowing they were just trying to be nice. Bethan and Alissa were friends, so the latter would have told her everything—or the part I didn't mind people knowing, anyway. But of course, there'd been so many witnesses to my abrupt de-glamouring when we'd caught the wizard, there was no way the boss wouldn't know what a public fool I'd made of myself by now.

And that wasn't even getting into the fact that my potential relationship with Nathan lay in tatters.

I wouldn't have said I had horribly low self-esteem,

but in the normal world, the only thing I'd win prizes for was faking my way through job interviews. Failure was second nature to me, but I couldn't remember ever feeling this wretched after messing up royally before. I'd lost more jobs than I had fingers on both hands, and I'd once been fired for accidentally downloading a virus onto every single computer in the posh London office I'd worked at as a recent graduate. Turning into a fairy in front of a bunch of werewolves was nothing in comparison, and Alissa was right—sooner or later, something else would come along and distract everyone.

I skimmed through the client list, crossing my fingers under the desk that none of the clients listed for the day had hairy faces or fangs. We mostly dealt with paranormal businessmen or fussy wizards. The tricky stuff was off-limits to me until I became better at witchcraft, unicorn-tamers being one of them. Luckily, today didn't seem too heinous, and neither did the small mountain of paper-work I'd accumulated. If anything, I needed the distraction.

The morning passed swiftly enough, and nobody asked any awkward questions over the phone. Routine was good. Mid-morning, however, Veronica entered the office. Tall and lean like her daughter, she had long silver-white hair and a manner that vacillated between concerned professional and eccentric.

She dropped some papers onto the edge of my desk without ceremony. "Do deal with this one as soon as possible," she said, looking distractedly out the window. "I have an important call to make."

I blinked after her as she left the office. "Something up with her?"

"Possibly," said Bethan. "I don't know, I think my dad may have got in touch with her again. She always acts slightly off when she gets a call from him, and she's been behaving weirdly since Saturday."

The normally straight-laced boss's one sore point was her ex-husband, the shifter who'd fathered her only child. And that was all Bethan had ever said on the subject.

I picked up the top page of the stack she'd put on the desk. "Guards? They want more security guards?"

"After the last few weeks?" said Lizzie. "I don't blame them."

"It doesn't say who's hiring them. Maybe the covens." My heart fluttered uneasily. Nathan, former paranormal hunter, was the town's only professional security guard. That they wanted to hire more came as no surprise, even though the mad wizard was in jail and the monster from the forest had met a swift end at the jaws of my pet cat. The boss likely didn't know that Nathan had jailed my father and that we hadn't spoken since he'd broken the news. Nobody really discussed his past as a paranormal hunter, including Nathan himself most of the time. It wouldn't be a bad thing for more security guards to help him out. The main reason we'd had so few dates was because everyone had wanted to hire him. Not that it mattered now.

"Sure you want to handle that one?" asked Bethan, eyeing the paper stack.

"Yeah, no problem."

If nothing else, it'd give me the chance to find out a little more about what paranormal security actually entailed. After reading the job description, I understood now why it was so hard for them to find any more qualified people, which was why they'd ended up sending half their gargoyle police force to guard the forest when there'd been a monster loose in there.

"So how long has the town got by with limited security?" I asked, skimming the details of the possible candidates.

"You mean, one security guard?" asked Bethan. "A while. It's partly because of the forest. We have shifters on one side of town, vampires on the other, and witches… basically, criminal elements have a tough time getting close. That, and we're hidden. There are wards around the whole town. And now the gargoyles are always watching the northern border too."

I nodded. "Okay. Makes sense. Most of the people listed here are wizards."

I turned to the next piece of paper, and my heart dropped through the floor. Listed on the page was the address of the local segment of the paranormal hunters.

"They want to bring in the hunters?" My voice rose in volume, as much as I tried to keep it down.

"Seriously?" said Lizzie, her brows rising. "That's… not good."

"I can take that one if you like," said Bethan, though she looked worried, too. "Mum didn't tell me, but it makes sense that they might want outside help."

Were they Nathan's former co-workers? "Oh, no, I don't mind making the call." *It's not like he actually works for them anymore.*

"If you're sure," said Bethan.

I hesitated, my mouth dry, then called the listed number.

"Welcome to the Lancashire Paranormal Hunters Division. Please leave a message."

"Ah," I said, flustered. "It's Blair, from Eldritch & Co recruitment… we're looking for some security guards for the village of Fairy Falls, Lancashire. If any of your employees are interested, please call this number and let us know."

I hope they aren't. Thinking of how certain paranormals, like the werewolves, reacted to Nathan… bringing actual hunters in would cause more strife when we really didn't need it.

I hung up and met Bethan's questioning stare. "Guess they're busy."

"Paranormal criminals don't catch themselves," she said.

"I guess not," I said. "So… what do you have to do to get yourself locked up in their prison? I heard it's worse than the town jail, even."

"It's for serious career criminals," said Bethan. "Or people nobody else wants to deal with."

"But don't a lot of paranormals police their own?" I asked. "I mean, we just saw that the vampires took care of the guy who bit someone without permission. And the werewolves deal with their own criminals as well."

"Yes, true," Lizzie said. "The hunters deal with criminals who don't belong to any paranormal community. Anyone from people who expose their magic to normals to paranormal serial killers."

Maybe that's what my father had done. Used fairy magic in front of humans. But it wasn't like they couldn't erase memories. And if he'd been jailed my whole life…

wait. *Idiot, Blair.* I should have asked Nathan *when* my father had been arrested. I'd been in too much shock at the time, but Nathan wasn't that much older than I was. He couldn't have been a security guard at the prison before I was born. And I'd only found out I was paranormal recently…

Which meant that up until not long ago, my father had been free, out there in the world, and had never got in touch.

I should have put that in the letter. I should have asked. I'd been too stunned that he wanted to get in touch at all to do some simple sums, but it sounded like he'd been free for most of my life. So why hadn't he wanted to contact me?

I had no idea how I got through the rest of the work-day, but the hunters didn't call back and I finished the rest of my client list with time to spare. I walked home in a daze, ignoring a fresh wave of stares from passers-by. Including schoolchildren, who added pointing to the mix.

"Fairy!" a little boy said.

"Is that the fairy witch?" a young girl eagerly asked her mum.

Wonderful.

I kept my head down, unable to believe I'd somehow found a reason to feel even *worse*. If I wanted to know more about my dad's arrest, I'd need to speak to Nathan again, but I couldn't face that. I still had a magic lesson to get through.

I reached my house… and found the cherry on top of the cake of the crappiest day ever. Blythe, my former co-worker, waited on my doorstep.

"I need your help, Blair," she said.

2

My mouth fell open and sort of hung there for a bit. Blythe, the former Dritch & Co employee who hated me since the moment we'd met, wouldn't ask for my help if there was a vampire chewing her face off. More to the point, we hadn't spoken much since I'd got her fired for hexing Callie, not to mention trying to get *me* fired for being half fairy.

"Blythe, what are you doing here?" I asked.

"I…" Her brow furrowed. "I need your help, Blair. It's urgent."

"You hate me." There was no other way to put it. Blythe and I might apparently be distantly related on my mother's side of the family, not that she actually knew that, but she'd made my life hell when I'd first started working at Dritch & Co, and tried to sabotage my relationship with Nathan. If I ever expected her to show up on my doorstep, it was to gloat, not ask a favour.

"I don't hate you," she protested. "I need your help. Can I come in?"

A growling noise came from behind me. Sky wound around my ankles, positioned himself in front of me and hissed at Blythe. It was lucky for her that he remained in his normal cat-size, but that growl said it all.

Blythe stumbled back off the doorstep, fear flashing across her features. "I'm not here to hurt you!"

True. My lie-sensing powers were infallible, as far as I knew. She wasn't here to hurt me… not in a physical sense anyway. But in an emotional sense? All bets were off.

"What is it, then?" I asked. "Are you really Blythe?"

"Yes, I am," she said quickly. "Why wouldn't I be?"

"Uh, because you're acting like a stranger." Unfortunately—or fortunately—my lie-sensing powers told me that she did, indeed, believe she was actually Blythe. "All right, tell me what it is." Maybe then she'd get out of the way of the door so I'd make it to my magic lesson on time.

"I'm… well. I'm under a curse," she said. "I think. I can't use my powers."

I blinked. "What, your mind-reading abilities?"

She dipped her head, her eyes wide. "Yeah. Totally gone. I can't hear a thing."

Not a lie. But what in the world did she expect *me* to do about it? "Er, you know I'm not actually a detective, right? Also, and I reiterate, you hate me. You put my co-worker under a spell, you tried to sabotage my job, you nearly got the wrong person jailed for murder…"

Her forehead crumpled. "I suppose I did. I'm sorry."

"Okay. You're either an illusion or pranking me, and I have to get changed for my magic lesson. Please get out of the way."

"Of course!" She gave me a smile worthy of Helen,

ambassador for the magical academy, and stepped aside. Blythe had never smiled at me in her life. I was pretty sure her facial expressions had two settings: smirking and scowling. Maybe my lie-sensing powers were faulty. But the footprints she'd left in the mud were real. Illusions didn't leave footprints, right?

Illusion or not, maybe she'd go away if I left her there. Checking the time, I gave up on the idea of changing and fed the cats before transferring my wand and keys into my smaller bag. Sky wove around my legs as I did so, unusually affectionate.

"Is it definitely her?" I asked him.

"Miaow."

"Nod or shake your head. It's her?"

To my intense surprise, he dipped his head a little. Hey, maybe the cat and I were improving our communication channels after all.

"Is there such a thing as a personality transplant spell? Wait, why am I asking you that? You're a cat." I shook my head and walked to the door, letting myself out of the flat.

Blythe was still outside, waiting beside the doorstep. So much for that idea.

"Er, I have a magic lesson to get to," I said. "Tell you what, come with me. You can ask Madame Grey or Rita to help you with your magic."

Maybe they'd be able to tell me if she'd been replaced with a super-nice clone or was just pranking me, so I'd have at least one problem taken off my hands. Of course, my magic lessons were a task and a half on their own. I was still in basic classes despite having cast spells that ought to be beyond my level. Let's just say I had a few issues with moderation. And focus. And not dropping my wand.

I kept one eye on Blythe as we walked in case she hexed me from behind, but she didn't even seem to have her wand on her. When we reached the witches' headquarters, however, it was to find the door to the main coven meeting room locked with a sign proclaiming yet another important meeting was in process. When I checked the classroom where my magic lessons usually took place, Rita had left a note on the desk apologising for not being there, but the covens had called yet another security meeting.

I shouldn't be surprised. The local witch covens ran the town—headed by Madame Grey and the Meadowsweet Coven—so they were taking most of the backlash from the near-war between the vampires and werewolves.

"Bad luck," said Blythe, but not in the snotty tone she'd normally have used. "I've never heard of anyone losing their magical powers out of nowhere before. That's why I wanted your help."

"I'm possibly the person least qualified for this, Blythe, to be honest," I told her. "I wouldn't know how to block anyone's powers."

Except when I'd blocked people from reading my mind. But that was an accident and I didn't know *how* I'd done it. I definitely couldn't stop people from using their innate powers. Hadn't thought it was possible.

Each witch had one major talent they didn't need a wand to use. Sometimes it ran in the family, sometimes not, but generally you could expect people closely related to one another to have the same type of talent. I still didn't know if my ability to tell a person's paranormal type was a witch ability or a fairy one, nor my lie-sensing talent. I'd temporarily lost my ability to sense lies once when a siren had used her magic to befuddle me, and it hadn't been a pleasant experience, so I understood why Blythe was panicking, even if it made zero sense for her to be so nice to me. I might not *like* Blythe, but if she was in a talkative mood, it wouldn't hurt to get the story from her.

"Tell me when it happened. Were you using magic?" I asked.

"No, I just woke up like this—on Saturday," she said. "I tried asking people, but well... they wouldn't talk to me. That's why I picked you, Blair."

I frowned. "They wouldn't talk to you? Anyone?"

I had to admit, if she was as pleasant to everyone else as she was to me, it came as no surprise that she'd made a few enemies. But that meant if someone had cursed her, it might have been anyone in the town.

Assuming I believed her.

She sniffed, and to my total astonishment, tears glittered in her eyes. "I can't hear their thoughts, not like I used to. I knew they hated me. I *wanted* to switch it off, sometimes, but I couldn't, and now I want it back."

"Oh," I said. *Nope. Blair, don't even think about pitying her.* She was probably putting on an act. A very convincing act, and who knew, maybe it *was* possible for someone's powers to be turned off. Considering how many people she'd probably alienated, maybe someone had decided to do everyone a favour. But turning off someone's magical powers didn't change their personality —did it?

"Er, have you been near the lake in the last two days?" I asked. "Or seen any… sirens?"

She shook her head. "No, not since before those awful murders in the forest."

Hmm. Sirens could walk on land, but I wouldn't have thought they'd come this far from the lake. Especially as it would mean going too close to the forest where the wizard's pet monster had attacked a bunch of elves. No… most of the people Blythe had made enemies of were human, as far as I knew.

I checked the time. Alissa was working until seven, and we were supposed to be going out socialising to ease me back into hanging out with the other witches for the first time since I'd been revealed to be half fairy. The last thing I needed was Blythe tagging along for the ride. I just wanted her gone.

"What do you think I can possibly do to help?" I asked her.

"Just… come with me and talk to my family. They don't know who might have done this to me, either. My mum's furious."

"Your family?"

She nodded. "Yes. I moved back home after I lost my job."

Oops. No, I definitely wouldn't feel guilty for that. And I didn't. Sympathy, though? I had way too much of that to spare.

Also… as Veronica had heavily implied once, Blythe's family were distantly *my* family too, on my witch mother's side. Maybe they'd even know why Tanith Wildflower had left town, met a fairy, and never came back. Or even how my dad had wound up in jail. Let's face it, I was more likely to get a potential answer from Blythe's family than from sitting at home feeling sorry for myself.

Whatever the reason, I found myself saying, "Okay, I will. I'll come and talk to them."

I deserve some seriously good karma for this.

Blythe remained in her weird mood during the walk. What was the word? Oh. Cheerful. I'd never seen her act like that in all the time I'd known her. It was possible she wasn't as prickly when she was around her family, but logic told me that her weird personality issue must be connected with her missing mind-reading abilities. Unless someone had hexed her twice. Or I was walking alongside a realistic illusion. Or dreaming. Nope, that would require actually being able to sleep properly.

"Why is everyone looking at you?" Blythe asked as we walked.

"I'm a fairy," I said. "You were one of the first people who worked it out."

"I know, I remember."

She hadn't been hit by an amnesia spell, then. She'd just… changed. People did change sometimes, but she'd been pretty set in her ways when I'd met her, and I'd thought she *liked* being mean to people. I knew better than to expect someone like her to change overnight. But maybe I was being too harsh. I was generally a fairly forgiving person, and holding grudges wasted too much energy for me to be bothered by it. Even with Blythe, we'd mostly stayed out of each other's way in the weeks after she'd been fired, and we'd never actively sought one another out.

"Mum, it's the fairy," said a little boy, staring up at me with wide eyes.

"Why does she look like a witch?" asked a small girl who was presumably his sibling. "She's not one."

She's not a witch.

A lead weight formed in my stomach. Kids said mean things thoughtlessly—I knew *that* from my stint as a nanny—but I wished I'd stayed in bed all evening instead. Leaving the house accompanied by my former mortal enemy was probably not the best way to re-induct myself into paranormal society as the resident witch-fairy freak, but I couldn't hide away forever.

Instead of ducking my head, I attempted to smile at the passing family. The little girl fell over her feet in an effort to get away.

Note to self: do not terrify small children.

I tried a smile on the next family with the same result. Maybe Blythe and I had *swapped* personalities. I gave up trying to smile and walked on, relieved when we left the crowds behind and Blythe finally stopped at a nice big house set apart from its neighbours by a high fence. While it wasn't quite as fancy as the vampire lords' houses I'd seen, it rivalled Madame Grey's house for size, and hers had four separate flats in it.

Of course Blythe would have money as well as looks, magical talent, and a terrible personality to boot. How had she ended up with everything while I'd wound up stranded in NormalsVille with no money or contact with my birth family? Especially with us being distantly related? *Well, if there's anywhere I might get answers, it's here.*

Blythe unlocked the gate, then meandered down a stone path to the front door. I hovered behind her as she let us into the hall, unsure what to do. I felt like this was the sort of house you took your shoes off in. The house

Alissa and I rented from Madame Grey might be huge, but it was lived-in. Everything here was so… shiny.

"Rebecca!" called Blythe. "I brought a visitor."

"Go away," said a female voice from a staircase off the hallway.

"That's nice."

Silence followed from upstairs. "Sibling?" I guessed. "You have a sister?"

"Yes, she's my little sister. My mother remarried after divorcing my father, so I have two older siblings who left town, too. Mum must be in the garden."

"Are you sure she'll want to speak to me?" I asked hesitantly. I *had* got Blythe fired, even if it'd been her own fault, and Blythe had also said that her mum was mad about her losing her powers.

"Sure," said Blythe. "I'm sure the two of you will be able to think of an answer."

I doubt it. New Blythe had entirely too much faith in me. Unless it was a side effect of the weird personality change, though—it didn't sound like Blythe had actually enjoyed reading everyone's thoughts as much as I'd thought. As herself, she'd revelled in plucking out my innermost thoughts and using them to humiliate me. But I was glad that ability had skipped me by. While there were a few situations where it would have really helped to know what people were thinking—like when I was trying to figure out how to break it to Nathan that I was half fairy, for instance—I couldn't imagine having the ability switched on all the time. Even the vampires could control whether or not to read specific thoughts. Vincent had told me.

Thinking of Blythe with a family and her own problems kind of blew my mind, to be honest. Despite my trepidation, I followed her through the hallway and out into the back garden.

The garden was stunning, a maze of wildflowers tamed into rows amid sprawling oaks. A woman sitting on a deck chair turned to squint at us through dark glasses. She looked exactly like an older version of Blythe. It was always weird when that happened in families. They had the same pale features and dark hair, the same willowy build, and the same scowl—not that Blythe wore hers at the moment. They even had the same walk, as I noticed when she rose to her feet. Even Veronica and Bethan didn't look that much alike.

"What are you doing in my house?" she asked, eyeing me as though I was a slimy slug on the lawn.

"I invited her," Blythe said quickly. "This is Blair."

Her eyes narrowed. "You're Blair Wilkes."

"Er. Yes. You must be Mrs... er." I should have asked Blythe's surname.

"Mrs Dailey," she supplied, looking at my half-outstretched hand as though I was offering her a dead pigeon. "What are you doing here?"

"Well, Blythe invited me, but you know what, this was a bad idea. I'll leave."

"Hold on," said Blythe. "Mum, you know Blair's a detective, right?"

"I'm not a detective!" I wished I could glamour myself invisible on the spot. "Blythe told me someone switched off her powers. Since, er, we have similar abilities, I wondered if you might know how it might have happened."

"Similar?" she echoed. "I think not. We don't do business with fairy filth."

My mouth dropped open. "Excuse me?"

Her wand was suddenly in her hand. "Don't you dare corrupt my family."

"Mum!" said a breathless voice, and a tween girl ran outside, looking panicky. "Don't shout at her. She's Blythe's friend."

"Er, no... argh." The words dried up in my mouth. "I mean, I came here to help Blythe. Did you know she's having trouble with her magic?"

Rebecca frowned. "What's the problem?"

"Nothing," said Mrs Dailey sharply. "Rebecca, go back to your room. Blythe, please escort Miss Wilkes away from our house."

Rebecca ran back inside the house without looking back, while Blythe hovered awkwardly on the side.

"But—" This was ridiculous. "Look at your daughter. She's acting weirdly. Do you think she might be under a spell?"

Mrs Dailey gave me a blistering glare. "If you dared to cast another spell on my daughter, you had better undo it, Blair Wilkes."

I swallowed. "I swear, I didn't do anything to her. We haven't even seen each other in ages."

"You cost my daughter her job. I won't let you take her magic away from her either."

"It wasn't her!" Blythe exclaimed, visibly alarmed. "I brought her here because I thought she could help me. I woke up without my magic and I know Blair has similar powers, so I thought she might know how to fix me."

"Enough. I'm calling someone who will take care of this little problem."

Ack. She was going to call the coven. "They're in a meeting!" I said. "Wait, shouldn't you be with them?"

Her eyes narrowed. "I'm not a part of the magical council, and I certainly don't need to waste my time with *them.*"

I backed towards the door into the house. "But aren't you in a coven? Like my mother was?" *Shut up, Blair.*

"Certainly *not,*" she said. "Your mother exiled herself from the family coven when she went chasing after fairies. And I have no intention of joining another coven again."

"I don't understand—" I broke off as she gripped her wand, and a few warning sparks shot out the end. "Okay. Sorry I couldn't help. Bye."

I pretty much sprinted back into the house and through the hallway, Blythe following more slowly. So now I knew why Blythe had hated me so much at first— not to mention how she'd known I was a fairy. Her mother had known Tanith Wildflower, and it did *not* sound like they'd liked one another much.

"Are you okay?" asked Blythe.

"Yeah," I said, thoroughly unnerved. "Really, I'm fine. I can get home alone."

Whatever was going on in Blythe's family was none of my business—even if you discounted the fact that her mother hated me, Blythe herself was acting like a stranger, and I had absolutely no clue whatsoever as to what might have messed with her mind-reading powers.

"Sorry about that," said Blythe. "I don't understand why she doesn't like you."

"*You* didn't like me up until whatever happened between the last time we saw one another and this evening," I said to her. "What did my mother do?"

Blythe shook her head. "I don't know. She left before I was born—your mother did. She left town. And my mum told me that she was trouble. I believed her because... I don't know. I believe everything she says."

Truth, said my lie-sensing power.

Hmm. Despite her weird behaviour, the opportunity to learn any clues about my past was more than welcome.

"Tell you what,' I relented. "If you wake up the same tomorrow, come and see me after work. We'll talk to the coven and get the spell taken off you."

"It wasn't a spell," she insisted. "I would know if it was. I just woke up like this."

"And was anyone else in the house? Might your mother or sister have done it?"

"Mum wouldn't," she insisted. "She's going to be seriously mad at me if I can't get my powers back."

Truth. "And your sister?"

"She doesn't have any magic yet," Blythe said. "Or a wand. She's a late developer, I guess. Mum has enough trouble dealing with her without adding my problems on top of it. Now she's mad at *both* of us."

Wow. Rebecca didn't have magic? In a magical town, that must be a serious struggle even without your own family looking down on you for it. Wait, why was I feeling even sorrier for Blythe and her family after this? Her mother had kicked me out of the house for trying to help. I was clearly in an over-sensitive state after the emotional rollercoaster of the last few weeks. I should get out while

I had the chance. I certainly wouldn't be going near Blythe's house again.

Tomorrow, one way or another, I'd get this case off my hands and go back to happily ignoring Blythe from afar. Blythe had always been better at holding a grudge than I was, and with any luck, she'd be back to normal soon.

3

I reached the house to find a young woman outside, moving a bunch of boxes into the hall. Tall and curvy with strawberry blond hair, she shifted another box aside and turned to face me. "Hey! Sorry about the mess."

Oh, new upstairs neighbour. Our last one had moved out after she'd been hit by a knockout spell meant for Alissa and me. We didn't speak to the others much—all of us worked at different hours and the flats were self-contained. Even Alissa's and my section of the garden was private, for our own use.

"Hey," I said, casting my mind around in an attempt to remember what Alissa had said her name was. "You're Nina, right?"

"Yes." Her gaze followed Blythe's retreating form, the hint of a scowl masking her otherwise pretty face. "You're Blair?"

"Yeah. Let me help you with those." I held the door open to make it easier for her to shift the stack of boxes into the hall, and then helped her carry them up the stairs to the flat above ours.

"Thank you," she said. "You live downstairs?"

"Yeah, I live with Alissa. Madame Grey's granddaughter. You've probably met."

"A couple of times." A brief silence followed in which she gave me the look I'd seen entirely too many times over the last week or two. My heart sank. *All right. Ask if I'm a fairy. I know you want to.* "Uh, I know it's not my business," she said. "But are you friends with Blythe?"

I blinked. Not the question I'd expected. "No, definitely not. I was helping her with something today, but we're not friends."

She wrinkled her nose. "Good."

I frowned. "Any reason?"

"Sorry, that was rude. It's just that we're not friends. She was awful to me when we were at school."

"Oh. Sounds like her, yeah." I decided not to mention the curse. With any luck, it'd be gone tomorrow, and her weird personality glitch along with it.

Nina shifted some of the boxes over the threshold into the flat. "She was particularly nasty to anyone who didn't develop their magical gifts until later on. I was thirteen when mine showed up, so she bullied me for two years straight."

"That's awful. Sorry." My brief shred of sympathy for Blythe evaporated. "She was horrible to me when I moved here, too. She used that mind-reading power of hers to get all my secrets and then spread them around. Did she do that all the time?"

"She did until my ability kicked in," she said. "Turns out I can neutralise others' powers. So, er, if your magical skill stops working for a bit, don't panic. It's not permanent."

Neutralising talents? *Hang on...*

"Oh, that's cool," I said. "I've never met anyone who can do that before."

She smiled. "It's not the most convenient power, I admit. Mum and I ended up leaving our original coven because of it to start a new one. Madame Grey helped us a lot."

"I didn't know you could switch covens," I said honestly. Every time I thought I'd got the hang of being paranormal, a new surprise came along. But Nina seemed nice enough.

"It's not common, but we kept clashing with our former coven's leader. It was inevitable. Anyway, I've a lot of unpacking to do. Nice to meet you, Blair."

"You too." I headed back downstairs. Blythe a bully... no surprise. Did Nina know she'd lost her powers? Perhaps. But as our conversation had made clear: it was none of my business.

I let myself into the flat and found Alissa sitting on the sofa, with Roald curled around her arm.

"Hey," she said. "I managed to escape work early. Got bitten by a patient and had to check into my own place of employment."

"Are you okay?" I sank onto the empty spot on the sofa. "Not a vampire, was it?"

"Nope. An elf," she said, grimacing. "It wasn't a venomous bite, at least... you weren't at a magic lesson, though, were you? I thought my grandmother was presiding over another coven meeting."

"Yeah, she invited everyone, including Rita, so my

lesson was cancelled." I reached for a cookie from the box on the coffee table.

"I did wonder," she said. "They're run off their feet because of the security issue. Last I heard, they were debating over whether or not we need to bring outsiders in."

"Oh, we had to deal with some of that at work," I said, having entirely forgotten my new dilemma in the wake of my encounter with Blythe's family. "Someone hired us to contact the hunters, so I might have to deal with them tomorrow."

Her eyes went wide. "The—*hunters?* Wow. They must be serious."

I bit my lip. "I guess they want to make sure this place is as secure as possible. I got the impression it was someone from the covens who asked us to get in touch, but the boss didn't say who hired us."

Was it Nathan? Surely not. I'd thought he'd moved to Fairy Falls to get away from the hunters, but it was possible I'd read the situation all wrong. Wouldn't be the first time. I mean, I'd assumed he didn't know I was a fairy when he'd really known all along.

"Yeah." She yawned. "I don't know, ask your boss. Where've you been all evening if you didn't have a lesson, anyway?"

"Blythe," I said, "has had a personality transplant."

"She what?" said Alissa blankly.

"She was being weirdly nice to me and came here asking for help. Then I got to meet her mother, and found out why she had such a grudge against me when we met. Seems she and my mum really didn't get along."

Alissa sat up, accidentally dislodging Roald in the process. "Blair, slow down. You met Blythe's mother?"

I bit into the cookie. "That's the weirdest part of this?"

"Yes, it is. I thought she left town."

"Apparently she came back." I explained Blythe's disappearing powers and perplexing family situation.

When I'd finished, Alissa said, "Wow. I assume the missing powers and her weird personality switch are linked. Maybe someone tried to get rid of her magic and got rid of her nastiness at the same time."

"Or the other way around?" I shook my head. "Through what, a curse or a hex? Or a spell? I don't even know where to start, but she thinks that I'm a detective and that I can help her. Also, she wasn't lying. Not a word."

Nor her especially nasty mother.

Alissa leaned back against the cushions, stroking Roald. "Yeah, that's bizarre. I'd dump her off on the coven."

"I would have done if they'd been available." I rolled my eyes. "I didn't know that accidentally catching a couple of murderers would mean even my enemies would try to hire me to solve their problems. At this rate, I'll get a job offer from Steve the Gargoyle by the end of the week. And I *have* a job."

"And magic lessons," she put in. "Unless you're desperate for a distraction, but seriously, getting involved with Blythe in any capacity is bad news. How do you know she's not putting on an act—right, the lies. But you know, it's not faultless. Your power."

"I know." I said. "I have to admit, it'd be kind of nice if that change was permanent. She wasn't even mad that I got her fired and caused her to have to move in with her mother again."

"Okay, that definitely doesn't sound like Blythe. From what Bethan told me, she was glad when her mother packed up and left. And she was *furious* to lose her position at Dritch & Co."

"Yeah, I got that impression," I said. "But who could have hexed her? Pretty much everyone hates her. Does she even have any friends at all?"

"I think she does," said Alissa, pursing her lips. "Bethan told me. But I guess we don't run in the same circles. I don't know. You didn't tell her you'd help her?"

"I said I'd take her to Madame Grey tomorrow." I gave a helpless shrug. "She's all weird in that state. Like a lost puppy. Anyway, her family... something isn't quite right about them. Her mum's like an older and eviler version of her—well, the person we used to know, before she pulled a Jekyll and Hyde. She threatened to call the coven on me. I'm sure Madame Grey wouldn't have backed her up, but she still seemed a little unhinged."

"You're telling me," said Alissa. "Yeah, I wouldn't go near her family if you paid me. I'm kinda confused on why you went over to begin with."

"I had a weird moment," I said, taking another cookie. "It's been a long day, and she was just—there. If the witches hadn't been in a coven meeting, I could have shoved her at one of them and let them handle it. I didn't know it was possible to switch off someone's powers." Except the new neighbour's ability, but she'd said it wasn't permanent.

"It's possible, but like you said... anyone might have done it. And if it's a curse, the caster—"

"Needs to reverse it," I finished, as Sky butted into my leg. "Sky didn't bite her, he just hissed at her. I took it to mean she wasn't plotting against me, at least."

The real question: what had come first, the personality change or the missing powers? Did it matter, anyway? Blythe and I would never be friends, and I wouldn't get any more involved in this than I had to. The best idea for now was to lie low and thoroughly avoid dangerous situations.

Sky butted my hand again. I leaned over to pet him and spotted a piece of paper tucked into his collar.

My heart jumped in my chest. With shaking hands, I removed the paper from his collar and unfolded it. The last few notes I'd received had been written in the same handwriting, which I assumed belonged to my dad—including the note warning me about Peter the wizard's plan to use me in his ritual. *How* he'd known about that, I'd never found out. But this note—the writing was different. It also wasn't written in English, but in some symbols I couldn't read.

I held the note out. "Er… Alissa. Any clue what this is?"

She took the piece of paper from me. "Huh? Blair, this is written in Elvish."

"Elvish… as in, elves?"

"Yeah." Her brow furrowed. "That's weird. Are you sure Sky meant that for you?"

"Is he roping me into solving the elves' problems, too? No, thanks. The last one I met wasn't particularly nice to me."

It'd been weeks ago, when I'd accidentally trespassed near their part of the forest. Apparently, the local elves had worked with Mr Falconer, the former wand-maker, who'd taken wandwood from their trees in order to make his custom wands. According to Rita, they were tricksters, and you didn't want to get on their bad side. Common opinion said they hated witches. Fairies, though? Well, they could have sent me the most grievously insulting letter ever and I couldn't understand a word of it. If this was a prank, it'd backfired spectacularly.

"The last one I met bit me," Alissa said. "I'd say get a translator, but I don't know any Elvish."

"Likewise." I gave the letter another scan and passed it back to Alissa. None of the symbols was even remotely similar to English. "Is this Blythe's new thing? Trick me into certain death by elves?"

"Elves aren't usually inclined to hurt humans," said Alissa. "They just prank us. Not that I'd want to go into their forest at any rate, especially after that monster killed three of them. And Blythe definitely wouldn't either, if she's got any sense."

"I thought they hated the witches," I said. "Why would they send *me* a note?"

"Because… they know you're a fairy?"

"Didn't they already know?"

She shook her head. "Haven't a clue. Just speculating. You exposed your fairy magic for the whole town to see, and to be honest, nobody would have guessed you were a fairy beforehand without using a detection spell."

Or my paranormal sensing ability. "Yeah, well. I was glamoured. I still am. This isn't my real face."

She put the paper on the coffee table. "You didn't look *that* different. Look… Blair, I don't want you thinking I see you differently now. I don't, not at all. And the people who really matter won't either."

"There's so much *staring*," I admitted. "Little kids run scared from me. Everyone looks at me as though I'm a circus freak, and I'm still *wearing* my glamour. I want to go out and pretend things are the same, but they aren't."

"They will be," Alissa said confidently. "Give everyone time to wrap their heads around it, and I promise, things will be back to normal. Besides. Don't forget you were the newbie not long ago. You're still a novelty for that reason alone. Not everyone cares that you're a fairy."

"The people who matter don't," I said, mirroring her earlier line, and a lump grew in my throat. My boss and co-workers didn't. Madame Grey and Rita had known from the start. None of them had treated me any differently. But—Nathan had mattered, too. And... he'd *said* he didn't care I was a fairy, not as much as he cared that I'd lied to him. But I hadn't heard from him since. Nothing, not a message or call. Admittedly, the main reason we'd been seeing so much of one another to begin with was because he'd been appointed as my bodyguard during the mad wizard's quest to kill paranormals for his own gain, but still. Maybe he was waiting for me to get in touch. But I'd already apologised for not telling him the truth, and he was the one who'd left *me* with a bombshell and a half to deal with. Namely, that he'd imprisoned my father.

Sky moved in front of the note on the coffee table and looked expectantly at me, as though he thought I had a translator lying around somewhere. Or an English-to-Elvish dictionary.

"Can *you* read it?" Elves and fairy cats didn't seem like they had a lot in common, but what did I know? "Who even gave you the note?"

"Miaow."

"You know I can't understand a word you say, right?"

"Maybe it's the same for him," said Alissa, getting to her feet and going to the bookcase. "He thinks you're talking nonsense. I swear my grandmother had an Elvish dictionary, but I have a feeling it's at the witches' place. Hmm."

"Another thing to do tomorrow," I said, rubbing my eyes. "On top of work, magic lessons, and handing Blythe over to someone else so she can annoy them instead of me."

"All in a day's work." Alissa yawned. "You know, I feel like staying in tonight."

"Me too. Want to order takeout?"

At some point I needed to re-induct myself into para-normal society as a fairy as well as a witch, but I wanted nothing more than an early night. And no drama.

———

A flash of glitter woke me from sleep. I blinked, disorientated, and a tapping on the window drew my attention to the little pixie on the other side of the glass. It was still dark outside. I squinted at the pixie, which hovered, beckoning urgently.

"What?" I hissed. "You want me to come outside?"

The pixie kept beckoning. Yawning, I climbed out of bed and put slippers and a dressing gown on. Then I grabbed my bag with my keys and wand inside it. Careful not to wake Alissa, I tiptoed out of the flat, then down the hallway to the doors leading to the communal garden.

Our section of the garden was on the right, and contained mostly herbs Alissa grew, with some wildflowers. I'd meant to set up my own space, but hadn't found the time yet. The silence made me a bit uneasy, despite the house's comforting presence behind me with its security wards. Thick trees sheltered beds of flowers, and—there was no sign of the pixie.

"Blair Wilkes," said a voice below my knee.

I jumped a foot in the air. Lurking in the bushes was a small pointed-eared man wearing brown-green clothes. An elf.

"What—what are you doing in my garden?"

"Are you Blair Wilkes?" he asked, in a loud, shrill voice.

I shot an alarmed look at the house. "Keep the noise down. People are sleeping in there. Where's the—wait, did the pixie let you in?"

The pixie appeared above me in a flash of glitter, bowing to the elf. I rubbed my forehead, wishing my brain would come up with less bizarre dreams so I could actually rest for once. "Cool. Pixies and elves partying in my garden. Don't wake me next time."

A sharp jab in my shin made my eyes fly wide open. The elf had *kicked* me. "What the—?"

"Do not speak that way to me, human. Are you Blair Wilkes?"

"Yes!" Ow. My leg throbbed with pain. So I wasn't dreaming. Or Blythe's madness had infected me, too. Wait, her sort of madness didn't involve pixies and elves camping out in my garden at five in the morning. Nobody except me had a life *that* bizarre. "Why are you here?"

"I have been tasked with issuing an invitation to one Blair Wilkes, to come and meet with our king at dawn."

"Uh... what?" I rubbed my shin, realising belatedly that

I was probably being rude. "Did you leave a letter with my cat?"

"Yes. Since you didn't reply, the king saw the need to send me to ask you in person."

I put my foot gingerly down on the grass. "Why?"

The elf drew himself up to his full four-foot height. "Accept the invitation and you will be granted passage into my kingdom. Decline, and you will never be welcome again."

"But I don't even know what I'm agreeing to!" I protested. "What does the king want to talk to me about? Is it because I'm a—" I broke off with a look at the pixie. "Can you understand him?"

"Yes." The elf sniffed. "Pixies are simple creatures, but this one seems to have appointed himself your bodyguard."

And the pixie was also in touch with my dad. "Is he telling the truth?" I asked it. "I'm not agreeing to go into the forest if there's another monster loose, or a mob of elves waiting to skewer me."

The elf gave me another jab, this time in the other shin. "Impertinence!" he yelled, loud enough to make me wince. I hoped the windows on the other flats were thicker than they looked. "You are a rude, ungrateful human. It is an honour to talk to the king."

I swallowed. Ticking off royalty didn't count as 'staying out of trouble'.

"I apologise," I said carefully. "I didn't expect to be woken at this hour by a visitor, and I wasn't able to read the note. Since, er, I've never learned the Elvish language. I'm from the human world."

"Yes, you are," said the elf sourly. "That is why the king

is interested to meet you. A fairy from the human world? It's unheard of."

I'm also half witch, and you don't like the covens. He must know that, but now didn't seem a great time to remind him.

"Yeah, I guess I am," I said. "Does the king want to see me because he's interested in whether I can do any fancy faerie tricks? Because, uh, I haven't known I'm a fairy for long enough to know much about my magic."

"No, he's interested to see you because he believes he once met a family member of yours."

4

Ten minutes later—I managed to convince the elf that he didn't want me meeting the king while wearing a pink dressing gown and fluffy slippers, so he let me go back into my flat to change—I set off for the forest, leaving a note for Alissa explaining where I'd gone. I took my phone with me, but I didn't want to wake her up by texting her. With any luck, I'd be back long before it was time to leave for work.

The elf followed the same path I'd once taken to the woods when I'd come to visit a witch who lived nearby, who'd actually been dating an elf at the time. I didn't know if they were still seeing one another, but maybe the elves didn't all hate witches. Or maybe the one I'd met the first time around had been an exception. Anyone would develop a dislike of wizards after dealing with the ex-wand-maker Mr Falconer. I was kind of surprised the elf messenger chose this route rather than the path near the waterfall, but this way was closer, and I still hadn't been back to the falls since the recent murders in the forest.

A thin mist hung over the trees at this hour in the morning, the sun peeking up behind the woods that stretched from the northern side of town to the lake. The pixie flew alongside me when the elf beckoned me into the woods off the roadside. Birdsong sounded in the background, the path as tranquil as ever, but doubts began to creep in.

"So... you know the fairies?" I asked my silent companion.

The elf didn't answer. He'd dangled the bait, and now here I was, following him into no man's land. The path dipped and ploughed into deeper woodland as we walked, until it hit me that we'd long since left the witches' territory behind. And he still hadn't said a word. The last time I'd talked to an elf in the forest, he'd yelled at me that my fellow witches were destroying the woods and I'd worried he might attack me. And as for the drunken one in the hospital who bit Alissa? Hmm. Maybe I should have reminded myself of that before committing to meeting the king. *This wasn't your best idea, Blair.* The trees were too close, their trunks gnarled, their branches twisted, like hundreds of faces watched me—

I nearly tripped over a tree root. There were elves *everywhere,* looking down from the branches, peering through bushes, all staring at me. It was a hundred times worse than being stared at by witches, and I'd come too far into the woods to run back out without ending up hopelessly lost.

"Er," I whispered to the elf in the lead. "Is everyone in the forest supposed to know we're here?"

"We're going into the king's lands," he said shortly. "Yes, I imagine they're curious as to why a human is here.

However, you had a direct invitation from the king, and you will not be harmed."

I can't believe this is my life. Imagine what the covens would say if they learned I was walking in the forest with elves. Then again, after I'd exposed my fairy side in public, nothing would shock people anymore. I could ride through the falls naked on a unicorn and nobody would bat an eyelid.

Finally, the leading elf stopped outside a large oak tree several times the size of a regular one, with huge branches reaching like giant arms, and thick roots sprawling across the forest floor. More elves stood in lines, wielding sharpened branches like medieval soldiers carrying swords. They stepped aside, revealing a gap in the roots which opened into a sort of tunnel.

"Your king lives in there?" I asked the elf.

"He always has."

I'd heard the elves hadn't always lived here, but I wasn't about to challenge him now. Would I even fit into that tunnel? I wasn't especially tall, but the elves seemed to stop at four or four and a half feet.

The elf held out a hand to stop the pixie. "He cannot go in there with you."

With a flutter, the pixie flew onto a nearby branch, while the elf stopped to exchange a few words with the guards. They didn't look thrilled at the prospect of the pixie fluttering around outside, either, but they stepped aside and allowed me to follow the elf to the massive tree trunk.

Please don't let this be a mistake.

I walked in, having to duck my head under the low-hanging ceiling. While the tunnel was wide enough to accommodate several elves, I had to walk at a half-crawl, half-crouch, since the average elf was the size of a child. Hoping that I wasn't breaking some rules of propriety, I resigned myself to meeting the king while on my knees covered in mud.

After a bit, the tunnel opened up into a wide cave with bark walls. The edges were lined with guards and an elf wearing gold finery sat on a tree stump in the centre. He was the same height as the other elves, but appeared smaller when sitting down.

The other elves bowed. I was on the floor already, but the elf who'd brought me here jabbed me in the spine, causing me to lose my balance and face-plant. My face flushed as I raised my head, awkwardly wiping my chin with my sleeve and hoping I hadn't smeared mud everywhere. "It's, er, an honour to meet you, your majesty."

The elves' king said something in Elvish to the guards, then stood up. In this position, he was taller than me. "You are Blair Wilkes, the fairy."

"I—yes, I am." Best to keep my desire to be more witch than fairy out of this conversation. "You wanted to see me?"

"Yes." I squirmed uncomfortably, feeling his eyes taking in every inch of my mud-splattered, awkward human appearance. "No fairies have lived near Fairy Falls for a very long time."

"I know," I said, then wondering if it sounded rude, I added, "I only moved here a few months ago. I'm new."

"So you are. You stink of human nastiness."

"Uh… thank you?" Oops. No sarcasm, Blair. That wouldn't help.

"The last fairy who came to the falls also paid me a

visit," he said. "He came to ask a favour. I see you have his likeness, even with your human ugliness on the surface."

My throat went dry and the insult slid right off me. "You're talking about my... my family?"

"Speak only when I command," said the king. "You may be human, but there's potential in you, according to Bramble here." He indicated an elf who I recognised as the one who'd yelled at me when I'd been in here looking for the place where old Ava's wand had backfired.

"But—he said the witches were evil and so was I," I blurted.

"We have no love for the witches," said the king. "The devious ones who confined us to the woods and tore out our trees by the roots." The other elves whispered and muttered, getting riled up. Not good. I needed to change the subject.

"Okay, I know you don't like the witches," I said. "I just don't understand why you wanted to see me."

He narrowed his eyes. "I wished to see the fairy... but you look like a human."

"Oh. I... don't know how to remove the glamour." I'd only done so when I was unconscious and when I'd stepped under the Fairy Falls. And the pixie had re-glamoured me the last time. It wasn't like I'd had the opportunity to practise with an expert like I had with witchcraft.

The elf king made an impatient noise and let out a command in Elvish. One of the others snapped his fingers, and I slid awkwardly forwards, my body feeling—lighter. Wings beat, lifting me higher. I breathed in, and despite the confined space of the tree, the air tasted fresher, somehow. The smells were more fragrant. The ceiling brushed my head as I hovered, managing to refrain from flying away.

"There," he said. "That's better."

I wouldn't say I disagreed, but the indignity of being shape-changed against my will grated on me. "What was that for?" Oops. I hadn't waited to be asked before speaking, but this time he didn't comment. Instead, he examined me as though I was an interesting toy.

"I have a request to make," he said. "There's something I need, and you're just the candidate to bring it to me."

"Bring… what to you?" My voice rose in confusion.

"Bring me some pixie dust," he said.

"I… why? There's a pixie right outside."

"Not that kind," he rasped. "It's a plant. A rare one, and as far as I heard, the witches have the last of it."

"What, you want me to steal it from them? Why?" *Careful, Blair.* Refusing a monarch wasn't wise, but neither was stealing from the witches, who'd done more to make me feel welcome than almost anyone else.

"I would have thought you would have guessed," said the elven king. "If you bring me what I request, then I will assist you with contacting the man who visited me in the woods not so long ago."

"My dad?" I said. "Are you sure it was him?"

"That male is the only fairy who's come into our territory in the last few decades, human. It was several years ago, but he had your face."

He's telling the truth. Whatever the pixie dust plant was, it shouldn't be that hard to get hold of, right? Let's face it, hearing the elf king out was probably better than getting my cat to sneak in and out of the jail. Not to mention, getting the elves on my side could only be a good thing.

"I'll do it," I said.

"Then you may leave."

The pixie waited outside the tunnel, fluttering anxiously. The same elf guard as before escorted me through a different route among the trees, until the other elves faded into the background and stopped pointing at me. I hardly noticed. A chance to find out why my dad had been near Fairy Falls and had never visited me as a child? I wouldn't miss it.

I stopped, realising the elf had disappeared into the trees. The pixie hovered next to me, making chattering noises.

"Hey," I said to it. "Er… can you show me how to redo my glamour?

The pixie snapped its fingers, and the next thing I knew, I was on my knees in human form. My clothes were streaked with mud and my face probably was, too. Pushing my hair out of my eyes, I looked up. The pixie had disappeared.

I rose to my feet. Ah. I didn't know this section of the woods. Had the elf got me lost on purpose? If I kept walking, I'd find my way out eventually, but I might easily end up on shifter territory by mistake.

"Blair?"

I spun on the spot, my heart leap-frogging. Nathan stood on the path between the trees, looking bewildered.

"Oh. Hi." Had he seen me transform? Or was it the mud? He didn't like the elves… no, he'd once made a remark about a group of elves overstepping their boundaries and giving the witches trouble. And it was the look on his face and his tone of disdain that had convinced me he'd feel the same about fairies. At least I was re-glamoured this time.

"You're on shifter territory," he said.

"I am? But I can't be..." That sneaky elf. He'd dropped me on the wrong side of the border on purpose. "I was lost. I'll go back..." I walked awkwardly around him and then stopped, not having a clue where the path led.

"That way," he said, pointing. "I'm actually on my way to talk to the werewolves."

"You are? Why?" I cringed inwardly. He had no obligation to tell me anything. I mean, look at me, making deals with elves as though I had the faintest idea what I was doing. "Uh, never mind. I'll see you later."

I hurried along the path, mentally kicking myself. Shifter territory wasn't the place to stop for a friendly chat, but it would have been nice to talk to someone about what the elf king had said. But first, I needed to tell Alissa where I'd been and clean myself up before work. Oh, and figure out how to get hold of this pixie dust, which would first involve working out what it actually was. It might even be here in the forest. Most herbs and leaves the witches used grew here. I also had full access to the witches' stores, in theory, if I could get Rita's help. But it sounded too easy. Everything I'd heard since I'd moved here told me that the elves were pranksters at best, hostile at worst. And it was obvious that my novelty value was mostly at work here. Still... it wouldn't hurt to at least try to fulfil the elves' request. They didn't invite humans to speak to their king every day.

I got back to the flat to find Alissa had left a note of her own underneath mine, saying she was on an early shift. That postponed our conversation until later, which meant I had nobody to discuss the elf king's offer with before work. I should have thrown caution aside and talked to Nathan, despite everything… but I hadn't been ready to open those old wounds, especially on shifter territory.

I went to my room to find some clean clothes and found Sky snoozing on my bed. "I could have used your company out there," I told him.

Sky remained asleep. Rolling my eyes, I grabbed some fresh clothes and made for the shower. I might have looked a dishevelled mess in front of the elves' monarch, but that didn't mean I had to show up for work in the same condition.

This time, I hardly noticed the stares on the way to the office. My mind whirled with the elf king's promise. A way to get information on my father without dragging Nathan into my business again, or breaking paranormal laws by getting my cat to sneak into a high security prison… I couldn't deny it was tempting. I just needed to keep my word, make the elves' king like me a little more, and maybe he'd give me answers.

Even if it meant embracing my fairy side, without shame.

5

I arrived at Dritch & Co to find Callie hunched over the reception desk, a scowl on her pretty face.

"Callie, are you okay?" I asked.

"What?" she snapped.

"Nothing," I said, startled. "Is something wrong?"

"No," she growled, sounding more wolf-like than I'd ever heard her in her human form. Frowning, I went into the office.

Once again, Lena was absent, and the other two were already buried in work. Bethan was so absorbed in multi-tasking that it wasn't until I put a fresh cup of coffee on her desk that she looked blearily up at me. "Hey, Blair. I take it you haven't heard?"

"Heard what?" I asked, confused.

"Lena quit." She rubbed her eyes. "That means we'll have three people doing the work of four again, and my mother's taken the day off, too."

"She has? Why?"

"I don't know. She's acting *weird* lately. I don't know. But it's up to us to hold the fort here."

"Huh." I picked up the papers I'd left here yesterday. "Ah. Forgot… I might get a call from the hunters today. I left them a voicemail message yesterday."

"Who put them up to this?" Bethan asked. "Seriously, if my mother was here, I'd be tempted to ask if she definitely wanted us to go ahead with the decision."

"Put who up to what?" I said blankly, wishing I'd had caffeine before coming to the office. Even a shower hadn't woken my brain from the shock of my experience in elf territory. "Oh, you mean, who's the person who asked us to call the hunters? Didn't you say you didn't know?"

"My mother will know," she said distractedly. "I assume she was okay with the decision, but she's not making much sense lately. Usually these decisions go to the covens first, so the town's council can make an informed choice. I mean, we do need security. More than we already have. But the hunters don't have a great history with a lot of the town's paranormals."

"Oh, is that why Callie's in such a mood?" I asked. "I just came in and she grunted at me."

"Did that to me, too," Lizzie commented. "Yeah, I don't think we should be hiring hunter security guards without the boss's definite say-so. If it turns out the covens are responsible, then it's fine. But otherwise…"

"They haven't got back to me yet." But an uneasy feeling stirred inside me. Bringing in more hunters… would Nathan agree that it was a good move? For that matter, what in the world was he doing on the werewolves' territory this morning?

I turned to today's call list in an attempt to get my

mind firmly away from elves, Nathan, and anything fairy-related. The boss had left a never-ending list, but not a very well put together one. A lot of the names were wrong. And the job titles. Sometimes the people listed didn't exist at all.

"Is the boss losing her grip?" I asked after the third failed call. "She doesn't normally make so many mistakes."

"She doesn't normally make *any* mistakes," said Bethan in a slightly frazzled voice. "I'm having to correct all the details on mine, and if yours is half as bad, we're likely to be here until midnight."

"Same with you two?" asked Lizzie. "It's not like her to make so many errors."

It wasn't, but maybe the boss had as much on her mind as I did. Between the three of us, we made some headway, but not much. Mid-morning, we all agreed to take a break to compare notes and see who had the most accurate details.

"I had something I wanted to ask you two," I said. "Have either of you seen Blythe lately?"

"Blythe?" said Bethan, raising her eyebrows. "Nope. Of course not. I thought she was avoiding us all."

"Yeah, you're not going to believe what happened to me yesterday," I said. "She showed up at my flat asking for my help. Not only is she acting weirdly nice, she seems to have *lost* her mind-reading powers. I read the truth from her—no lies."

Bethan and Lizzie both gaped at me, their files forgotten.

"That wasn't Blythe," said Lizzie. "Was it? Are you sure someone—like Blythe herself—didn't just send an illusion after you?"

"Is she that good at illusion spells?" I said sceptically. I'd heard her mind-reading powers were the best magical skill she had.

"Well... no," said Bethan.

"Also, I met her family," I added. "They believed it was her. And her mum's even worse than she is, if possible."

"How in the world did you end up meeting her family?" asked Lizzie. "Nobody goes to her house. At all."

"She invited me." I shrugged, beginning to wonder if I should be telling them this. "Look, she was wandering around outside my house acting like a stranger. I was concerned. And we couldn't get answers from Madame Grey or the other coven leaders because they were all in a meeting, so I figured I'd hear her out. Didn't come to any conclusions, but she does seem to have lost her mind-reading powers."

"Okay, I get *that*," said Bethan. "As unlikely as it is, any of us would panic if our magic stopped working. And she viewed hers as the best thing about her, and so did everyone else, to be honest. But as far as the rest of it goes... nope. I'd say she's messing with you on purpose."

"That's what Alissa said," I said. "And I would believe her, but she seems so genuine. She didn't even bring up the fact that I got her fired so she had to move back to her mum's place, or any of the other arguments we had."

Bethan shook her head. "Well, that definitely doesn't sound like Blythe. From the hints I picked up when we worked together, she didn't get along with her family. I thought she lived with her dad and older siblings after the divorce before she got her own place."

"How do you even know that?"

"She let a few things slip when she worked here,"

Bethan said. "Yeah, sounds fishy. If she's not lying, then someone must have put a spell on her. Or used a potion. How long has she been like that for, do you know? Most potions have a limited span before they stop working."

"She said her mind-reading powers switched off over the weekend," I told them. "She just woke up like that. I assume the personality change is a side effect. Or the other way around."

"You can't change someone's basic personality," said Lizzie. "Except through something like an amnesia spell. If she still remembers who she is, it's got to be a surface charm. They don't last long, though. Not like curses."

I cast my mind around to remember my lesson with Rita about the differences between the types of magic cast with a wand. "Curses last longer than hexes," I said. "So if it's still there today, it's probably a curse."

Curses were the hardest type of magic to track because they could be cast at any time without the victim being aware in the slightest. They could also be put on an object or scheduled to switch on after a certain condition was met... the possibilities were endless. Which meant figuring out which person had decided to put the curse on her was as difficult as reading the boss's handwriting.

"Does it matter?" asked Bethan. "You aren't seeing her again?"

"I said I'd take her with me to the coven," I said. "There's no reason she can't go there herself, but she seems to have attached herself to me for some weird reason. Anyway, I already have a magic lesson tonight, so I figured it couldn't hurt."

Technically, I didn't have a lesson, but after yesterday's had been cancelled, I knew Rita would want to make up the lost time. And while my curiosity about the next stage of my witch magic remained, my mind was more on the elf king's quest and my need to find the pixie dust. Rita would be able to help with that. Or Madame Grey. The sooner I got it done, the sooner I could learn why my dad had left me alone in the human world.

Bethan sighed. "You're too trusting, Blair. Anyway. Let's get back to it."

———

When I got home, it was to find the door already open, and Nina standing there, looking furious.

"What is she doing in here?" Nina demanded. "Get her out."

"Who?"

I looked past her, through the open door. Oh, no. Blythe was in my *flat.*

"She's insisting you invited her over and won't leave," Nina said through clenched teeth.

"I didn't," I said. "I'll talk to her. Blythe, can you go to the witches' headquarters? I'll be there soon. I just need to drop off my work things."

She blinked brightly at me. "Oh, sure!" She bounded out of the hallway.

Nina gave her a glare before retreating into the building, while I waited outside to make sure Blythe actually walked off rather than hanging around outside. She headed down the road, after giving me another puppy-eyed look that was going to haunt me for the next hour.

Why can't one thing in my life go without a hitch?

I let myself into the flat and found Alissa lying on the sofa. "Rough day?"

She grunted. "What was that shouting?"

"Blythe was hovering outside the door. Didn't she knock?"

"I was asleep." She lifted her head up. "Who else was there?"

"Nina. If I didn't know her ability wasn't permanent, I'd say she's the one who switched off Blythe's powers. She does have the ability to do that…"

Maybe even my lie-sensing skills. But I'd sensed them still working when we'd talked yesterday, and I wasn't convinced they weren't a fairy skill instead of a witch one.

"What does that matter?" she asked.

"It matters because someone hexed Blythe to turn her personality backwards. And Nina has the ability to block others' powers."

Alissa's face scrunched up. "I have no idea, and to be honest, I don't care. You shouldn't either. You have enough problems without pulling Blythe's onto your list as well. And more to the point, what was the deal with the note you left this morning? Did you seriously go wandering into the forest?"

"Uh… yeah. I have a few new developments to tell you."

Alissa listened in silence as I described my journey to the elves' territory, the meeting with the king, and his offer to help me find my father in exchange for the pixie dust.

"Huh," she said. "Pixie dust as a plant? Never heard of it."

My heart sank. "Really? Did they send me after something impossible on purpose?"

"No clue," said Alissa. "Why do you have to do what he says?"

"Because he's met my father. I think. He didn't lie."

"Blair, you need to stop trusting these people. First Blythe and now the elves."

Alissa's lack of faith stung a little, but she was probably right.

"I'll ditch Blythe as soon as the curse is off," I said. "I know she can't keep showing up at our flat acting like a lost puppy. We have two cats and a pixie to contend with as it is."

"I didn't see a pixie."

"He was here this morning, with the elf ambassador. I wouldn't have gone wandering into the woods with him otherwise."

"At least you have some sense left."

"Thanks," I said. "What's up with you?"

"Long day," she mumbled, rubbing her forehead. "Might have picked up a fever from one of the patients. I'm going to get an early night."

Who knew, maybe I *was* making a series of monumental mistakes by trying to help Blythe and the elves' king. I'd ask Rita about the pixie dust, and if it turned out it was impossible to get hold of, I'd tell the elves I'd failed and leave it at that.

———

True to her word, Blythe waited outside the witches' headquarters and *beamed* at me. "You did come back." She blinked at me with her huge eyes. Lost puppy indeed. The real Blythe was going to be hopping mad when she came to her senses and realised what she'd done. That thought alone was enough to cheer me up. I walked into the building in higher spirits, imagining Blythe's look of dawning horror when it hit her that she'd apologised to me, brought me into the family life she kept hidden from everyone, and begged for my help.

Luck was with me today, and I found Rita in the classroom. She was a witch of around forty-something, with dyed curly red hair and an indeterminate number of bangles on each arm.

"Hey, Rita," I said. "I have a couple of things I wanted to ask you before my lesson."

"Oh, you have a lesson?" asked Blythe. "I'll wait outside."

"Or ask Madame Grey," I said to her. "She'll be able to help you."

"That's not a good idea," said Rita. "She's very busy. What did you want to ask her?"

Blythe looked questioningly at me. "Blair thinks something's wrong with me."

"Her mind-reading powers vanished," I explained. "At the same time, she started acting like... this. We used to work together."

Rita's gaze sharpened in understanding. "Yes. You're Blythe, right?"

"I am," she said, sounding worried. "Er, I'm not in trouble, am I?"

"No. Sit down. Let me try a few spells so I can see if anyone cast a curse on you."

Blythe sat obediently at the front desk, and Rita pulled

out her own wand, walking around her. "Hmm. No visible effects."

Her wand moved in circles, and Blythe fidgeted, her mouth pulling down at the corners. "What's happening to me?"

"It's not a spell," said Rita. "Nor a curse with any side effects that I can see. When did this happen?"

"Saturday, I think," I said. "She showed up at mine first thing Monday morning, thinking I could help. I don't know why. It's not like I haven't left a trail of unholy chaos behind me lately."

"You did catch a murderer the other week." Rita's lips pursed, and she stood back, waving her wand over Blythe once more. "Not a spell. Or a potion. I'd say a hex or curse, but that's a very odd combination. If I didn't know better, I'd say it was more than one."

"So someone wanted to get rid of her magic and someone else put the personality altering curse on her?" Were there *two* people out to get her at once?

"She might even have done it herself. Did you, Blythe?" She spoke to the baffled young witch as though addressing one of the academy's ten-year-old students.

"I don't *think* so," said Blythe, biting her lip. "Am I stuck like this?"

"I'm sure Madame Grey will be able to fix you when she has a free moment," said Rita. "Blair, did she give you any clues about who might have done it?"

"Well, she argued with my neighbour today. They didn't seem to like one another, or she didn't before the curse, anyway. Nina has the ability to turn off other witches' powers... but she said it was temporary."

"Oh, I heard about her," said Rita. "I'll ask her to come

in to have a word. Blythe, I'm afraid there's not much I can do for you. Blair and I have a lesson now."

Yes, we do.

Blythe obediently turned and left, and I shook my head after her. "She's seriously lost it. Not that it isn't an improvement, but it's plain weird."

"Madame Grey will sort her out," said Rita. "I apologise for missing your lesson yesterday. Have you practised the spells we learned with your left hand?"

Oh. "I… no. I've been busy. And I made such a mess of things in our flat last time that I didn't want to cause Alissa any more stress. I've been run off my feet at work, too."

I sounded like I was making excuses, but I'd genuinely forgotten. I'd hardly had a moment's peace for ages.

Disappointment clear in her tone, Rita said, "In that case, get out your wand. I'll leave a message for Nina asking her to come here so I can ask her a few questions."

I picked up my bag and carried it to my usual spot in the classroom as she made the phone call, trying to quash my feelings of guilt. I was only one person trying to live what felt like three lives. Besides, I knew at least one solution to my magical mishaps: use my left hand and not my right. Hopefully after that, success would follow.

I pulled out my wand, which I'd decorated with a pair of fairy wings. While it felt more at home in my left hand than my right and I was relieved to have an explanation as to why my magical skill was so erratic, I still wasn't a particularly confident spellcaster. Though now I thought about it, my magic hadn't malfunctioned since the killer's threat had gone. Hmm.

Rita nodded when I explained this after she'd finished

talking to Nina on the phone. "You were under a lot of stress. That can't have helped."

"Yeah…" I decided not to mention I was under almost as much stress now, minus the threat to my life. And that might change if I aggravated the elves. "Before we start, I wondered—do we have any pixie dust in the ingredient stores?"

"Any *what?*"

"Er, it's a plant, isn't it?"

She blinked. "Yes, I believe went extinct a few decades ago, at least. Madame Grey will know."

I nearly groaned aloud. Trust me to fall for a trick like that. "Never mind."

"Okay, Blair. Show me the levitating spell, using your left hand this time."

I was on my best behaviour for the rest of the lesson. So, thankfully, was my wand. Maybe having something else on my mind made it easier not to stress about magic. Of course, it didn't hurt that I was no longer agonising over when to tell Nathan the truth about being half fairy, which had distracted me for weeks. For the first time, I left the classroom feeling optimistic about my future as a witch.

That feeling vanished when it hit me that I'd have to either tell the elves I'd seen through their trick, or avoid them forever. I paused outside Madame Grey's office, debating, then I knocked. She was likely to know why the elf king might have asked me to bring him pixie dust. If it'd really gone extinct, the older witches might remember. Or Vincent the vampire might. As an elder vampire, he'd been around for much longer than the majority of people in town. But I'd tried to swear off dealing with the vampires any more than I had to. Partly for safety, partly because I wanted to stop accidentally ticking people off. I was incredibly lucky not to have run into any were-wolves when I'd ended up on their territory this morning.

Nobody answered my knock. Maybe she was out.

"Blair?"

I turned around. Nina had entered the lobby, letting the doors close behind her.

"Hey," I said. "Rita's just in that classroom there."

"Oh. What did she want to see me about?"

She hadn't told her? "Er, best you ask her yourself."

Rita stepped out of the classroom. "Don't worry, I just wanted to ask you a couple of questions."

Nina hesitantly followed her in. Since she didn't dismiss me, I did, too.

"Blythe?" she said, when Rita had explained her condition. "No. I didn't touch her. We haven't spoken since she showed up at Blair's flat." Her mouth pressed down at the corners and my lie-sensing ability told me she was being honest. It seemed to be working as normal, then.

Rita asked the same question a couple of times using different wording, with the same result, then dismissed both of us.

"The snake," said Nina, as we left. "She's trying to frame me. I bet she put the curse on herself to get sympathy."

"Maybe," I said doubtfully. "I don't think she did put it on herself. She liked using her power too much. She has so many people who dislike her, anyone might have done it."

"Who can blame them?" Her brow creased in disgust.

"Where *is* Madame Grey? I haven't seen her since the weekend.

"You haven't?" I asked. "I was kind of hoping to speak to her."

"About what?"

"Have you ever heard of a plant called pixie dust?"

"Pixie dust?" she echoed. "No. What type of plant is it?"

"A lie," I muttered. That's what I got for trusting the elves. Rita would tell me as much. I wouldn't get answers here—and finding out more about my family would have to wait.

6

I woke up the following morning in a foul mood. Alissa was dead to the world and grumbled at me to go away when I knocked on her door. Hoping she didn't sleep through her midday shift, I left for work alone, tired and frazzled. I ran into Nina on the way out, and while her hello was friendly, I had the distinct impression she wasn't happy about yesterday's questioning. She was likely innocent of cursing Blythe, but since Madame Grey hadn't been available and none of the other coven leaders were around, they hadn't been able to do a more thorough test to see if it was actually a curse that'd affected her, nor question her about everyone she'd annoyed in the last week or so. Blythe herself thankfully didn't ambush me this morning, at least.

But the day was gloomy, I had no pixie dust, and if I didn't give the elf king an explanation, he might send more elves to torment me. I definitely wouldn't get answers at work, so I shoved it out of mind and went into the office.

"Hey, Blair," said Lizzie. "There's a problem. The boss is missing."

"Veronica's *missing?*" I asked.

"She hasn't spoken to me since Monday," admitted Bethan. "That's not like her. At all."

"Nor is what she did to the files yesterday," said Lizzie. "She's always so efficient. Puts us all to shame."

Bethan shook her head at the stack of papers on her desk, her brow pinching. "She won't answer her phone. I don't think there was anything wrong with her yesterday, she just took the day off for no apparent reason."

"Have you been to her house?" asked Lizzie.

Bethan moved the haphazard stack of files. "No. But when she doesn't answer the phone, it usually means she's not at home. It's weird."

"Let's check her office, then," I suggested.

There wasn't much else to do. Leaving the files behind, we headed for Veronica's office door behind the reception area.

"What're you doing?" asked Callie grumpily.

"Checking what the boss left in her office," said Bethan.

Callie grunted. "Didn't she leave it at your desks?"

"Not all of it," said Bethan, half to herself. "This isn't right. Callie, when did you last see my mother?"

The receptionist twisted in her seat and scowled at us. "Why?"

"I'm concerned that she's not coming to work and hasn't been seen all week," Bethan said.

"Shouldn't you be more concerned with actually doing your jobs?"

It wasn't like Callie to be mean. At all. "What's wrong with you?" I said. "If you've seen her, why not tell us?"

Callie gave me another scowl. "If you really have to know, the last time I saw her was when Blythe came here on Saturday. The boss came out of her office to stop me from ripping her throat out."

"Blythe was *here?*" I asked. "On Saturday? Are you sure?"

Saturday. That was when she'd woken up without her mind-reading powers... and when her personality change had presumably taken place as well. Why come to the office? To ask for Veronica's help or for her old job back, maybe?

"Didn't you hear what I said?" asked Callie. "Now, stop badgering me."

"Okay..." I followed Bethan into the boss's office. A moment later, Lizzie joined us. "Did she leave anything in here?"

The decor of the office was plain, the furniture bare and austere. Usually it changed to match the boss's tastes on that particular day, but she hadn't been in here since the weekend.

"I'm looking," Bethan said, moving to her desk. "What she was actually doing here on Saturday, I have no idea. I was out."

"I don't think Callie's in the mood to chat," Lizzie said quietly.

I shook my head. "Maybe it's just a coincidence. But Blythe changed personalities around the same time. Now Veronica *and* Callie are acting seriously off—the only two people from the office who worked at the weekend. Callie seriously didn't sound like herself just then."

"No," said Lizzie. "You're right, Blair. But… why would Blythe put a spell on herself?"

"Who knows?" I said.

"I am *not* using a spell on a werewolf to find out if she's under a curse or not," said Bethan, rummaging through the boss's desk drawers. "Her family would tear me to shreds. Anyway, maybe she's suffering from out-of-season full moon blues."

"That's a thing?"

She slammed the papers on her desk. "I have no bloody idea if it's a thing. If Blythe *did* hex my mother, I'm not letting it slide. Where is Blythe's house, anyway, Blair?"

"I wouldn't go there," I said. "Her mother was seriously mean."

"*My* mother is missing," she said. "I'm going to check her call history and see who she last spoke to, because it definitely wasn't me."

"Okay." I sensed Bethan's temper brewing, not because of a curse, but because she was worried. If Blythe had come here for revenge, maybe she'd cursed the boss and it'd backfired on her, but I'd thought she wasn't a very powerful witch aside from her mind-reading powers.

"I'd have thought Veronica would have bested her if Blythe tried anything," I muttered to Lizzie as we re-entered the main office. "She's a much better witch. Even if Blythe got lucky."

Lizzie frowned. "Yes, she is. Maybe someone else got both of them. The office has less security at the weekend. Only Callie."

"And it looks like they got her, too," I added. "But that doesn't explain why Blythe came here to begin with. If she's the one who did it, maybe she caught herself in the spell by accident."

"Maybe," said Lizzie. "If all the files are inaccurate and Veronica is missing, should we even be trying to contact clients today?"

"Exactly what I was thinking," I said. "It seems wrong to just… leave, though. Maybe we should ask Madame Grey if any of the other witches have seen the boss lately. Or maybe she's having one of her weird eccentric moments and she'll be back later this afternoon like nothing happened."

Lizzie and I looked at one another, then at the stacks of papers on our desks. The mountain of work wasn't going to finish itself. But with the boss's notes inaccurate and the woman herself absent, none of us had a hope of getting through four people's mismatched work.

"Come back over here!" Bethan called frantically from the boss's office. "Guys, you want to hear this."

Lizzie and I ran to join Bethan, who stood over her mother's desk with her phone in her hand.

"What is it?" I asked.

"She called Blythe… no, Blythe called her." She frantically dialled. "Blythe was the last person she spoke to. No messages… I'll have to call her. Unless—Callie, what time did Blythe show up?"

"Would you all shut up?" Callie growled. "First thing in the morning. Why?"

Bethan shook her head, putting the phone down. "I don't know what this means. Did Blythe hex her? Maybe this is her revenge on us for firing her."

"And she managed to put the spell on herself as well?" I

said. "I guess—I can see that. But what did she actually *do* to Veronica?"

"She didn't leave a message," said Bethan, her expression distraught. "Blythe... it can't be a coincidence that she was the last person to call here."

"Is that the only call the boss took this weekend, though?" asked Lizzie. "Maybe Blythe was visiting and someone else cursed all three of them?"

"What, just paying a friendly social call?" I said sceptically. "I don't think so. Remember last time we thought there'd been a break-in and Blythe turned out to be responsible the whole time? Why should this be any different?"

"Fair point." Bethan's face was set. "I'm calling her. And then I'm calling Madame Grey. She'll have Blythe's number in here somewhere."

She dug into Veronica's desk drawer, presumably for her list of contact details of past employees. I doubted Blythe would be able to offer an explanation in the state she was in now, but Veronica's disappearance was alarming, and all the more because it coincided with Blythe's own transformation. And Callie must be under the same spell, somehow. It didn't add up at all.

After Bethan dialled Blythe's number, Lizzie and I waited with bated breath. Then—

"Not in," said Bethan, her jaw tightening. "All right, I'm going to find her in person."

"Hang on," I said. "Rita already said it wasn't a spell with obvious external effects. We'd have to get her or someone else to come and check on Callie to see if it's the same. And shouldn't we maybe try to find your mother first? Even if she's cursed, she must be somewhere in town. Otherwise, Blythe might easily claim that we're lying and we wouldn't be able to prove otherwise."

"Mum was acting weirdly enough that she might even have left town," said Bethan. "She kept talking about my dad. You know, the guy she's hardly spoken to since he cheated on her and they divorced."

"What do you want?" Callie's voice growled from reception. I spun on the spot, thinking she was speaking to one of us—but she held the reception's phone in her hand. "You're not welcome here, hunters."

Hunters. Oh, no.

"I said, you're not welcome here," the werewolf snapped.

"Er, Callie," I said hesitantly. "Is that the paranormal hunters' division?"

She turned on me, her eyes narrowing and turning alarmingly wolf-like. "Yes. Did you set these monsters on me?"

I raised my hands, stumbling back a step. "The boss asked me to contact them about security. Want to hand the phone to me? I'm the one who they need to speak to. I can clear this up."

Without warning, she let out a half-animal roar, dropping the phone as she did so. For a brief, desperate moment, I hoped the call had disconnected, then I heard voices on the other end, too muffled to tell what they said.

Oh god.

I lunged for the phone, but Callie got there first, transforming into a wolf in one swift dive. One second she was a blond woman, the next, a huge furred beast with teeth dripping with drool. Reaching out a huge paw, she crushed the phone into the carpet.

I swallowed hard, my gaze darting from the smashed phone to Bethan and Lizzie trapped in the boss's office behind us.

"Callie?" I whispered.

She let out a low growl, then removed her paw from the phone and jumped over the desk, landing on all four paws.

"Did someone trap her in wolf form again?" I whispered. "Blythe—damn, I knew it."

"No, I think she shifted on purpose," Bethan whispered back.

The boss was gone, and now we'd managed to tick off the paranormal hunters, who probably thought we had a wild werewolf in the office.

I'd been wrong. Things absolutely *could* get worse.

"Callie," I said. "Please, shift back. If your family thinks we're responsible—"

The wolf dived over the desk, kicking it over, and growled in my face. I tripped backwards over my own feet and fell in a heap on the carpet. With a final growl, Callie jumped over the desk and padded to the doors, shouldering them open and stalking outside.

The three of us stared after her. Nobody gave chase. A person couldn't catch up to a werewolf on foot, and with the mood Callie was in at the moment, we might get injured. I should call the hunters back and explain that Callie was under a curse and wasn't herself, but somehow, I doubted they'd buy it.

The doors opened, and Nathan walked in. His gaze went from me, half sprawled on the floor, to Bethan standing frozen in Veronica's office, the overturned desk, and the smashed phone.

"What happened here?" he asked.

"Callie." I pushed to my knees, my legs throbbing from where I'd skinned them on the carpet. "She shifted and ran. Someone hexed or cursed her... and possibly the boss, too."

"Someone hexed her into wolf form again?" He strode to the desk and turned it the right way up. The simple practical motion seemed to wake the others up, and they came out into the reception area.

"No," Bethan said. "Someone put a mood or personality altering hex or curse on her, and I think they did the same to my mother. I haven't heard from her since the weekend, though."

"Personality altering... in what way?" For some reason, he was looking at me. Maybe he thought I was responsible again. In fairness, I didn't blame him.

"Callie was acting seriously grumpy," I explained. "Then she just—snapped. But the reason we think it's a hex or curse is because someone did the same to Blythe over the weekend as well. And Veronica, too, I guess. I don't suppose you've been to the witches' place lately? We need to get Madame Grey involved at this point. None of us can fix this."

"I can help fix *this*," Nathan said, indicating the mess on the floor. "Except the phone."

"Oh, god," I said. "The hunters... they're coming here."

Nathan's eyes widened. "The hunters—why?"

"They were on the call list for this week, for security," I said quickly. "So I left them a message. They phoned us today and Callie picked up right before she..." I trailed off, gesturing helplessly around. "They're going to come after her, aren't they?"

His mouth tightened. "The hunters won't come into the town without Madame Grey's say-so."

"But she's been in coven meetings all week," I said, my heart sinking fast. "I'm sorry. Veronica left them on the call list and I thought it was odd, but I didn't know she wasn't acting like herself at the time." To my horror, tears stung my eyes. It was too much—all too much. If I had to admit it to myself, the reason I'd called the hunters was to prove to myself that I wasn't afraid to go near Nathan's history even if the man himself wasn't speaking to me. And now I'd messed that up, too.

Like it or not, though, Nathan was the only person around who might be able to solve at least one of our problems—namely, that his former employers now thought there was a mad werewolf on the loose in our office. The hunters weren't exactly known for being benevolent towards disobedient paranormals. We needed to clear this up.

Nathan picked up some of the papers and put them on the desk. "Which office called, do you know?"

"I have the number on my desk, but obviously..." I pointed at the smashed phone. "Not sure if they were the ones who called. I don't know what they said to her before she snapped."

"You three should clean up this," he said. "I'll call the hunters myself. They know me, so they won't act hastily if I explain there was a mistake."

"I hope not," I said. "Callie's been through enough trouble thanks to Blythe already."

"Are you certain Blythe did it?" he asked.

I nodded, then shook my head. "The thing I don't get is that she was the first person affected. I thought someone hexed *her*. She's acting weirdly nice, and her mind-reading powers stopped working. I assumed the two are connected, but Callie doesn't *have* magical powers."

"Looks like her shifting power is working fine," Lizzie put in. "Really weird. But it must be Blythe. Veronica and Callie were both in the office when she visited, and that's the last time any of them were acting like themselves."

Nathan looked around the reception once again. "All right. Clear up the office, and I'll call the hunters."

He was actually going to stick around and help us? Even after I'd royally screwed up? Admittedly, we knew less than Nathan did about the hunters' likely reaction to Callie's growling down the phone, and he was probably the only person apart from Madame Grey who could stop them showing up here and threatening everyone.

Lizzie, Bethan and I cleaned up the office and left the boss's most recent assignments in her own office for her to deal with whenever she came to her senses. It wasn't ideal, but better than leaving the place in chaos. To my intense surprise, Nathan stuck around to help, though it was clear that staying was pointless if none of us would get any work done. It was best to wait until the boss came back before trying to make sense of the notes she'd left in her absence.

"I'm going to my mother's house," said Bethan. "I'll call Madame Grey while I'm at it."

"Yeah, I'll come with you if you need me to," said Lizzie.

"Me too," I put in. "I need to talk to her as well."

And if not? Blythe was the only option.

The two of them left, and I belatedly remembered I'd

left my bag in the office. I ran in to get it, and ran out to find Nathan standing in the reception area.

"Er, I'll see you around," I said clumsily.

"Are you going home?"

I half shrugged. "No. I don't know where Madame Grey is at this time, but—"

"She'll be in her office, I imagine," he said. "I'll walk you there. I doubt Callie is a danger to anyone but herself, but there's a reason the town's rules discourage shifting in the streets."

"Anyone who was outside just then must be terrified," I said. "Can't say I blame them, but I hope her family doesn't decide I'm their number one enemy again. This time it wasn't remotely my fault."

"If it's clear she chose to shift of her own accord, they'll probably assume she wants to be left alone," he said. "Unless this... curse has other effects as well?"

"I have no idea," I said wearily. "It might not even be a curse. But a spell or potion would have worn off by now. Curse or hex, cast by someone who hated Blythe, or by Blythe herself. Our theory is that she came into the office to confront her former employer and accidentally got caught in her own spell. Callie and Veronica were the only people here."

"Possibly," he said. "Or maybe the spell that blocked her powers was cast in self-defence. But I can't say I know enough magic to be sure that it isn't one curse, not two."

I rubbed my forehead. "I hope Bethan finds Veronica. It's not like her to just... take off."

"Yes, I hope she's still in town," he said. "The hunters listened to my explanation, but I can't say they won't send people here anyway."

I swallowed nervously. "Did they say they would?"

"No, but they said to update them on the situation in a day or two. They know shifters can be temperamental."

"I don't understand what Veronica was thinking, asking the hunters to be interviewed for security duty without consulting anyone else first," I said. "Someone hired us, but they didn't leave a name. If she knew who they were, then they must be okay, but she's not exactly in a great state for approving clients at the moment."

A furrow appeared in his brow. "I'll ask them who made the call, then. I should have done so earlier, but I didn't know."

"Sorry, I should have told you that before. I was kind of shell-shocked from Callie nearly swatting me with her giant paw."

"Why do these things always happen to you, Blair?" He shook his head.

"I could ask you the same question." Wait, why did I say that again?

"What do you mean?"

"I... well. You always wind up having to pull me out of whatever hole I've managed to fall into. I know it's not just me having to deal with this mess, but still. What did you come to the office for to begin with?"

He opened and closed his mouth again. "Initially? I had something to talk to your boss about, security-wise. But I also hoped I'd see you."

My heart dip-dived pathetically. "Why?"

Because he'd changed his mind? Because I hadn't messed everything up after all?

"I called the prison I used to work at over the weekend," Nathan said. "I asked them if they knew where your father had been taken after I brought him in. They refused to answer me."

"Oh." My brief thread of hope died. I already knew where my father was—thanks to his note. I weighed the odds, then said, "I kind of know where he is, anyway. My dad left me a note with Lord Goddard's pixie. Pixies can travel through walls."

Why not tell him everything? It wouldn't make any difference now. My dad was in jail, and we had bigger, more immediate problems to deal with.

"Lord Goddard's…"

"Pixie," I said. "He was at the old vampire's manor, hidden with glamour, and he appeared when we were in the room with the coffin. Pretty sure they were friends, or he was trying to stop Peter completing the ritual. It was the pixie who kept setting up those booby traps."

"Glamoured," he said, and I quickly looked away, not wanting to see if his expression contained curiosity or disgust. "Whereabouts is he?"

"Who, the pixie?" Oh. Wait. "Uh, you mean my dad? The LFPF. Alissa said it's a prison for paranormals."

"The LFPF?" His eyes widened. "Blair—that's the highest security prison there is."

"I know. It was my dad who left the note and wanted to speak to me at the solstice. I guess I have to wait until the next one to see him. Apparently, it's the only time he's allowed out."

"Oh," he said. "Yes… that sounds right. I'm sorry."

"Right," I said dully. "Wait—I don't blame you, you know that? I had no idea I was paranormal at the time, let alone that my family might be in jail."

"Of course," he said. "I just wish I could be of more help."

Uh... in what way. "Er, well, the hunters do kind of think there's a massive wolf on the loose in Dritch & Co's office. Who knows, maybe I'll get to question them in person."

His mouth pulled. "For all our sakes, I hope *not*. Not all hunters are likely to handle the situation in the same way."

"What, they'd... hurt Callie?"

"She sounded like a wild animal. And I saw the look on your face when I came in after she left. You were terrified. Most hunters would act first, ask questions later. It doesn't seem that that's their plan, but I'm intending to keep an eye on the situation."

My throat tightened. He still cared about me. *Duh, of course he does.* He'd wanted to give *me* space, not the other way around.

"So do you see this pixie often?" he asked. "Was it him you were with in the forest?"

"Yes..." Honesty was the best way forward from now on. "I was actually meeting with the elf king, who sent me an invitation and wouldn't take no for an answer. It wasn't really something I could refuse. Then his elf guard dropped me off on werewolf territory, but I didn't know. I swear I'm not trying to annoy these people, it just... happens."

He didn't need to know about the quest, because chances were, I was going to fail anyway. Pixie dust was extinct, and the elves probably intended to break their word regardless. There wasn't any need to endanger my own freedom and annoy the hunters. Who knew, maybe they'd label me a criminal by association.

He shook his head. "Don't play with the elves, Blair. They're known for pranking humans."

I'm... not human. My throat closed up, and while I didn't speak the words aloud, he seemed to hear them all the same.

To my surprise, he met my eyes with no judgement. I couldn't read the look in them, but it wasn't disgust or condemnation. "I can't say I've ever spoken to the elves' king. They don't have any issues with the hunters at any rate, because they keep to themselves."

Hmm. "Yeah. I'm not sure I'll be going back. That's the least of it all, anyway. I guess I need to see Blythe again, if Madame Grey isn't around."

"I'll leave a message on her phone," he said. "And we'll walk back that way."

And we did, side by side. For a moment, it was like old times, like when he'd walked me back from one of our dates. Okay, so most of them had ended in disaster, but he didn't hate me at least. Maybe things weren't so dire after all.

7

Once Nathan had gone, I skipped the rest of the way down the road, and then felt guilty for my good mood, considering Callie had sprinted off in wolf form, Veronica was absent, and Blythe... who knew where Blythe was. If I wanted answers, I'd have to confront her in person or leave the witches to handle her, assuming Madame Grey would drag herself away from the coven meeting for long enough. That Blythe had shown up at Dritch & Co's office at the weekend was surely no coincidence, and now the hunters were involved, it'd be the whole town's problem by the week's end if I didn't try to wrangle the truth from Blythe about why she'd really come to the office last weekend.

My phone rang. I got it out of my pocket, assuming it was Bethan, but instead found myself faced with an unknown number. I frowned. I didn't use my phone as much as I used to, since everyone in Fairy Falls lived so close to one another. I usually only texted Alissa—and Nathan.

"Hello?" I said.

"Hi, it's Louise. From the hospital. I just wondered if you'd seen Alissa today? She didn't show up for work."

"She didn't?" That wasn't right. "I haven't seen her since last night, but she claimed she had a headache yesterday. Maybe she has flu. I'm about to go into our flat now, so I'll see if she's there."

"Let me know," said the nurse.

I hung up and kept walking towards home, my heart sinking uneasily. *Please say the curse didn't get Alissa, too.* She *had* been acting grumpy yesterday, but everyone had off days. Alissa loved her job, so maybe she had picked up a virus from one of the patients, like she'd thought yesterday.

I opened the door and went into the flat. No sign of Alissa, or the cats. I strode over to her bedroom, pushing the door inwards. Her room was a tip, clothes spilling from drawers, her work uniform strewn across the bed. She'd even left her keys and phone in a heap on the floor.

"Alissa!" I shouted, running into the living room. "Roald? Sky?"

Sky was probably with that vampire again. Thoroughly alarmed, I grabbed my own bag and keys and then picked up Alissa's, too. Then I locked up and went upstairs to Nina's flat. Knocking on the door, I wondered how I'd ever thought things would return to normal.

Nina answered the door. "Hey, Blair. Something wrong?"

"Hey," I said. "Sorry to bother you. I wondered if you'd seen Alissa?"

"Yes." She scowled. "She left an hour ago and was quite rude to me on the way out."

My shoulders slumped. "I'm sorry. Our flat's in such a state and she left her keys behind so I worried someone had kidnapped her."

"Huh?" said Nina. "I saw her running past, with a broomstick, if that helps."

"A broomstick?" I echoed. "She doesn't have a broomstick. She told me…"

She told me she hadn't ridden a broom in years. Witches in Fairy Falls didn't typically travel by broom, partly due to the weather conditions, partly because everything was so close together. With one, very obvious exception: the High Fliers, the daredevil Quidditch players of the paranormal world. Alissa had told me when I'd first moved here that she used to be a member of their group, but had quit. I hadn't even known she still had a broomstick.

"Blair, what's going on?" asked Nina.

I shook my head. "Alissa—I don't know if I'm jumping to conclusions or not, but whatever spell hit Blythe got my boss, too, and one of my co-workers. And I think it might have got Alissa, too."

"Oh," said Nina. "I didn't know. Honestly."

Maybe she expected me to accuse her. And who knew, maybe her ability *could* mess with my own lie-sensing powers. But she'd have no reason to attack Callie or my boss.

"I think Blythe might have started it all and accidentally hexed herself in the process," I said. "Er—you haven't seen *her*, have you?"

"No, I haven't. Sorry."

"Okay. Let me know if you do. I'm going to look for Alissa before she does something stupid."

Once again, I ran from the building, clutching my bag containing Alissa's keys and phone. Maybe I ought to stop off at the hospital to check when they'd last seen her, but instead, I found myself switching on my levitating boots and hurrying through town to where the shapes of broomsticks were visible in the air above the lake. The boots were useful when I wanted to run somewhere without tripping over my own feet, and they'd be even more useful if Alissa was where I suspected.

I really hoped I was wrong.

I ran-floated between stone houses down the path to the lakeside. The lake glittered, its waters like spun gold under the sun, reflecting the broomsticks spinning above it in death-defying stunts.

I stopped by the bank, tilted my head back, and squinted at the distant stick-figures in the sky. They moved way too fast for me to spot Alissa from this angle, and flying into the middle of their formation might potentially cause a collision. They had enough accidents on their own, from what Alissa had told me, and she'd quit herself after a particularly bad one. Fliers often crashed into one another or fell into the lake and needed to be fished out. The lake itself wasn't exactly safe either, with biting water imps, sirens with deadly songs, merpeople and nereids frolicking in the shallows, and even a vampire pirate ghost Alissa and I had run into here once.

I trod from one booted foot to the other and watched the fliers, hoping that if Alissa was up there, she at least knew what she was doing. The High Fliers were a mix of witches and wizards, and while I couldn't judge from the ground, they seemed to have a system, flying in formation like a flock of birds. They never slowed, making it impossible to tell what each individual flier's face looked like. Nor could I see who led the group. Minutes crawled by, and I remained standing at the lake's edge, feeling vaguely stupid. They had to come down to earth eventually, right? I could sit down and watch the show, but then the whole day would disappear with nothing solved. I needed to know if Alissa was with them, and there was nobody on ground level to ask.

Eventually, the fliers slowed, hovering in lines in the air. One broom hovered at the front of the group. Their leader, I guessed. From what I could tell, she was female, and giving them a speech. Not the best time to interrupt, but it was the first time they'd slowed down.

I switched on my levitating boots and flew into the air. I'd look a real fool if it turned out Alissa wasn't up there after all, but it was the quickest way to check.

I spotted her almost immediately, her dark curly hair flowing behind her and her pose on the broom as casual as if she was sitting on a bench on the ground.

"Alissa," I said, but the wind was too loud, snatching away my words. "Alissa! Your boss wants to talk to you!"

"What are you doing up here?" asked the leader, a witch wearing a bright green pointed hat. It must be strapped to her head, considering she'd been flying upside-down and it hadn't fallen off.

"Er, sorry to interrupt," I said awkwardly. "I need to talk to Alissa. Her boss at the hospital wants a word with her."

"Well, don't be long," she said.

Alissa expertly wove her way out of the line and halted next to me, looking irritated. "Can't you leave me alone?"

"Alissa, listen, you're not acting like yourself."

"Says who?"

"You," I said. "You told me you weren't ever going to join the High Fliers again. You got injured last time. And you wouldn't walk away from your job for this, would you? I'm not joking, your colleagues are confused, and your boss will think you've quit."

"This is who I really am, Blair. This is who I want to be. Don't fly up here and spoil the fun."

"Alissa!" I pleaded. "Just come down and I'll take you to your grandmother. Then she'll be able undo the curse on you."

"I'm not cursed!" she said. "Just because you're no fun, it doesn't mean the rest of us want to stay on the ground forever."

"You *like* working at the hospital,' I said. "You even left your keys behind, you know that?"

"Who cares?" she said. "Maybe I don't want to live with you anymore."

It's the curse, I told myself, but my heart dived at her words as though I'd fallen off a broom myself.

"You're not yourself," I said, as much to me as to her. "The curse is talking, not you, and I'm not about to let my best friend get injured because of it. If you keep flying like that—look, you remember the accidents, right? You've dealt with them at the hospital enough times."

Her forehead scrunched up. "You're being a spoilsport. And you have some nerve lecturing me when you're always wandering around the forest on your own or hanging out with vampires."

I became conscious that most of the fliers were blatantly listening in. Great. I didn't need the whole world to know I'd been making acquaintances of elves and vampires. But getting Alissa back to earth before she injured herself mattered more than my own feelings. Madame Grey would never forgive me if she got hurt, and I wouldn't forgive *myself* if I didn't at least try to talk some sense into her.

"Besides," she said. "Not all of us have wings, or are afraid to use them. Some of us want to be more than we are."

That stung. "You're being ridiculous," I said. "I care about you not getting injured, Alissa, and I care about you screwing up the career you love. Just come down to earth and I can fix this, and I promise you won't regret it."

"Screw you," she said. "I don't want to talk to you again, Blair."

"You heard her," said another of the fliers. "Stop bugging her and go back to earth. Only High Fliers are allowed in this airspace."

"But she's under a curse," I protested. "She's not herself. She doesn't want to—"

"Don't tell me what I want, Blair," she shot at me.

"Look, I don't know you," said the flier, "but you're killing the mood and upsetting our newest recruit."

"Yeah, you are," said Alissa.

I knew I was beaten. "Fine, I'll wait down below. Someone's put a hex on her, and I'm going to undo it. We're friends, and we look out for one another."

I descended, humiliation searing my face as the High Fliers watched me drop out of sight. They didn't know Alissa, so it'd be a waste of time hanging around arguing with them. Besides, they might be reckless and irresponsible when it came to their own safety, but I'd done some fairly stupid things myself. Maybe Alissa had it right.

She's under a spell, and you'll undo it as soon as she comes down to earth.

I hadn't seen anyone else I knew among the group, so Veronica hadn't got the sudden urge to fly—meaning Bethan might still need my help. As for Alissa, she couldn't stay up in the air forever. Once I told Madame Grey, she'd probably levitate her granddaughter back to earth herself. I never had asked if she'd approved of her old hobby, but considering how overprotective she was of her other grandchildren, I'd take a wild guess that she wouldn't stand for this.

A few tears fell as I descended, swept away on the breeze. *Don't be ridiculous. It wasn't really Alissa who said that.*

But I couldn't help wondering... had Blythe taken away my best friend, too?

I flew to the witches' headquarters, using my boots to propel myself along the road. It struck me that using my wings would be quicker, if I ever had time to learn to remove the glamour myself. Maybe I *was* afraid to get my wings out in public again, but I'd caused enough of a scene today already.

Blythe's antics had gone beyond accidentally cursing herself. Eldritch & Co was in jeopardy, Bethan's mother was missing, Alissa had lost the plot, and there might be a team of hunters descending on the woods any day now. And it was only mid-week.

I skidded to a halt at the entrance to the witches' place, colliding with Bethan. "Ah, sorry!"

"Whoa." She caught her balance on the door. "Blair—what are you doing?"

"Same as you—came to see Madame Grey. Right? Is she in?"

"She's not there," said Bethan. "And my mum, idiot that she is, has left her security spells all over her house so I can't get inside. I don't think she's in, but who knows where she is?"

"I wish I knew," I said. "Madame Grey is going to kill me when she finds out Alissa defected to the High Fliers and has lost her mind as well."

"Alissa did *what?*"

"The curse got her, too," I said. "She ran out on her job and now she's zipping around on a broomstick. I didn't have the chance to ask if her healing powers were functioning as normal, but it doesn't matter. She's not herself."

"Alissa, Callie, my mother," said Bethan distractedly. "Alissa came into contact with Blythe recently too, right?"

"Since she showed up at my flat multiple times? Yep. I was going to look for her after we find Madame Grey. Suppose I can leave a message… wait." I dug in my bag. "I forgot, I picked up Alissa's phone and keys to give to her. I can call Madame Grey using Alissa's phone. If she won't pick up for me, she might for her granddaughter."

Bethan let out a frustrated noise. "I get that the covens are kicking up a fuss about security at the moment and that takes precedence, but my mother is *missing.*"

I turned on Alissa's phone and scrolled through the contact numbers. "Can't you use a spell to break into your mum's house?"

"She's paranoid, so nope. It's almost as well protected as your place."

"Blythe got in there easily enough," I muttered, thinking of Nina and her hostility. Of course she hadn't got into the actual flat, but—"Wait." I stopped mid-dial. "I may have a way to get into your house, but it involves my cat. I'll tell you after I call her."

"Your *cat?*"

"Yep," I said, distractedly, holding the phone to my ear. It rang a couple of times. Then came Madame Grey's clear voice: "You have reached the office of Madame Grey, leader of the Meadowsweet Coven and of Fairy Falls's Council."

"Madame Grey!" I said. "It's Blair. Your granddaughter is under a curse."

"You have reached the office of—"

Argh. It's a recorded message. She must have used a spell to record her own voice, because it sounded like she was actually there. "Madame Grey, please call me back. Your granddaughter is under a curse and might be in danger." I hung up, frustrated. "I can't believe this. I know she doesn't always answer her phone, but—"

Bethan made a small noise. "You don't think she—Madame Grey might have been affected, too? Has anyone seen her recently?"

"You know… I have no idea." If the leader of the witches had been hit, too? It didn't bear thinking about. "Oh, god. Is Rita in?" No, it was still the middle of the afternoon. Rita was at the academy at this time, tutoring the students.

"She will be this evening."

"Right." I returned my attention to Alissa's phone and skimmed through the contacts. I'd met her parents once, but considering Alissa's erratic work schedule, she didn't get a lot of time to visit them. They'd definitely want to know their daughter was under a curse. If I couldn't persuade her to get out of the air, maybe they would be able to.

"Blair, seriously, what was that about your cat?" Bethan asked.

"He can walk through walls," I said. "But I don't know if he'll do it on command. I also haven't seen him much this week, which is pretty normal. He'll come when I call him, though. Sky?"

Bethan blinked, baffled. "You know, Blair, I thought some of the stuff you did at work was weird, but this… is normal for you?"

"Normal? No such thing," I said. "But if there's anything you want me to get from inside your mum's house, Sky can probably find it."

"Wait, is Sky *the* cat? The one who caught the wizard?"

"Yep," I said. "Anything you need from the house?"

"Her phone, if it's there," said Bethan. "I don't know if anything else would do any good. There's no evidence that she left town, but if she's not home, she must have done. There isn't anywhere else she would go in town for three days without anyone seeing her."

"You think she went to find your dad? I know it's not my business, but…"

"I think she did," said Bethan, half to herself. "My dad is… wild and adventurous. If this curse is causing people to give into impulses, it'd explain why she did it."

"That happened to Alissa, but not Blythe," I said. "I doubt she ever had the secret desire to be nice to everyone."

That got a small laugh out of her. "No. But she was the first victim, wasn't she? And she did it to herself."

"I'm going to find her," I said. "Maybe I'll call Alissa's family… but I don't want to worry them unnecessarily. Especially if it turns out Madame Grey is fine."

Since the Meadowsweet Coven ran the village, her family was pretty extensive, but I hadn't met all her relatives. They lived pretty spread out, probably because they'd grown up under Madame Grey's thumb and had wanted to get away as soon as possible. The youngest grandchild, Sammi, was still at school. For her sake, I hoped nobody else in the family had been affected.

A drop of rain fell. Bethan looked up. "Uh, it looks like Alissa will be out of the air soon. Even the High Fliers don't fly in full-on storms. Did you say your cat was on the way?"

"He usually answers when I call him, but maybe he's busy doing cat things." I skimmed distractedly through Alissa's contacts again. Her mum was the person she talked to the most, based on the calls she took in the flat, but she rarely invited her parents over. She liked her independence, and joining the High Fliers when she'd turned eighteen had been her first act of rebellion against her family.

"Miaow." Fur brushed my legs, and Bethan jumped in alarm.

"Or maybe he'll show up now." I crouched to stroke Sky between the ears. "Sky, we need your help."

He sat and looked up expectantly at me. *Good, he's behaving today.*

"Can I pet him?" Bethan asked. "He doesn't look like most familiars I've seen."

"That's because he's... special."

Sky seemed to like that, stretching and purring as Bethan gave him a stroke. "Miaow."

"Sky, we need you to get into somewhere."

"Breaking and entering again?" asked a smooth voice.

This time, both of us jumped. Vincent the vampire stood on the path behind Sky as though he'd been dragged here by my command, too. So that's where Sky had been all day. The two had been friends before I'd even moved here, since Sky had used to live in the bookshop where the vampire spent his free time hanging around in the history section.

"It's for a good cause," I said.

Bethan had gone very still, her manner nervous. "Er… hello, Vincent."

"I don't believe we've met," said Vincent. "Blair's friend?"

"Yes, and co-worker," I said. "Vincent… We're borrowing Sky. For an important cause."

The vampire made me edgy and flustered at the same time. He looked like a human waxwork model, his features eerily perfect and chalk white, his hair glossy and black, and he tended to dress smartly in dark colours. I was pretty sure he liked to play up to the stereotypical vampire image on purpose. He could also read minds, so he'd likely figured out the situation the moment he got within hearing distance of us.

"Breaking into your own mother's house?" asked Vincent. "It won't do any good. Ms Eldritch left with her phone. I saw her talking on it when she left town."

"You… saw her?" asked Bethan, her voice faint. "Nobody told me."

"Er, she's under a curse," I said quickly to Vincent. "Or something similar. We think the same might have affected—"

"Keep it down," said the vampire in a soft voice. "It won't do to spread gossip if the leader of the covens really has disappeared. There are others vying to take her place."

"I… excuse me?" Talking to Vincent was like having a conversation with someone who was seven steps ahead of me. Mind-reading abilities were a serious perk, and his might even be better than Blythe's, especially as he could switch the ability on and off whenever he liked. I'd also blocked him from my thoughts a couple of times, but since I didn't know how I'd done it, I assumed my mind was pretty much as open as anyone else's. He must know Madame Grey was missing and had drawn his own conclusions.

"You don't think the council have held so many meetings for fun, do you?" queried the vampire. "Many disagree with how Madame Grey handled the matter of the vampires and the werewolves' conflict and the murders in the woods. They think those events were a wake-up call for the town and that new leadership should step in. I imagine those people would be thrilled to know their leader is incapacitated."

"Wait—who?"

Vincent turned around, as though he'd heard something on the breeze, and disappeared.

"Vincent!" I yelled, but he'd gone.

"Did you just shout at a vampire?" Bethan said.

"Gah!" I knelt down on Sky's level. "Can't you bring him back?"

"Miaow."

No, I guessed. Just great. I squeezed my eyes shut, feeling a headache brewing. "He's *on* the council, the town council at least. Who would want to unseat the leader of the witches? Would one of them have—wait, are Blythe's family involved?"

"How should I know? I can't even find my own mother." Bethan groaned in exasperation. "Right, let's assume he knows Madame Grey is gone. If she is…"

"Nobody's in charge?" I said. "She was definitely here yesterday, right? There was a meeting on. Unless it happened today. Wait—that's when they got Alissa. She was a bit grumpy last night after work, but it was only this morning when she lost her head and ran off."

"And they all came into contact with Blythe," she said. "Are you sure it's her? Because if it is, it'll be kind of hard to bring her in for questioning when the person in *charge* of questioning witches who break the law is missing."

"I wasn't sure it was her, not at first," I said. "But she's the one connecting factor between all the people who've been affected by the curse. I can't think of anything else they have in common. Or how it hit so many people at once."

"Yeah," she said. "You know where Blythe lives, though, right?"

"Yes, but her mother threw me out." She also hadn't struck me as someone who might make her daughter's magic disappear on a whim, given how furious she'd been. "She hates me, because of something to do with my family. She also insinuated that she blames *me* for cursing her daughter. If we show up at her house, she'll chase us off."

"Do you have Blythe's number?"

I shook my head. "The number we had at work didn't get through, did it? I guess we could go and knock. Her mum might not be in, since it's in the middle of the work day. What does she even do for a living?"

"You think I know? I thought she left town." Bethan sighed. "She used to work for the council a few years ago, but she doesn't hang out with the other witches. At this point, I think Blythe might be the only person who can give us a clue about what's going on."

She was right, but I didn't want to go anywhere *near* Blythe's house. I looked down at Sky, who'd stretched out in one of his 'stroke me' positions. He yawned as I ran the tips of my fingers down his spine. "Sky, can you get Blythe to come and see me?"

"Miaow." He didn't move.

I rolled my eyes. "He was keen to help when it was my life at stake, but I'm one of the handful of people who's seen Blythe lately and *hasn't* been hit by the curse." That alone seemed odd in itself, but without knowing what form the curse took, or if it actually was one, we had no more clues than before. I'd be a fool not to at least try to speak to Blythe again. She was where this had all started, after all.

9

Bethan and I climbed the hill to Blythe's mother's house, going over our theories again so many times that it made me dizzy. The raindrops continued to fall infrequently, but since it hadn't turned into a proper storm yet, the High Fliers' brooms remained in the air. From this height, they were visible above the forest, a mass of tiny dark shapes in the sky like a flock of distant birds.

Blythe *must* be involved. But while her mind-reading powers had gone, none of the other affected people had said theirs had. Not that Alissa would have used her healing powers up in the air unless she fell off her broomstick, and Veronica hadn't stuck around long enough for anyone to check whether she'd suffered any other side effects. Until Alissa got back on the ground, there wasn't anyone else to question.

"I'm sure my mum's powers stopped working," said Bethan. "Did you see the state of the files in the office?

She didn't even spell *my* name right. Normally she can fill out twelve at once."

"Fair point," I admitted. "If not Blythe, though, I suppose anyone might have come into the office on Saturday… that must be when Veronica got hit, because they got Callie, too. I don't know how Blythe expected to be able to hide from this."

"Hitting herself with her own curse was a good way to hide it," Bethan said wryly.

"Except for the bit when she didn't lie," I added. "She knows my power, though, and I bet she knows how to get around it. Out of character or not, she's still the same Blythe."

We reached her family's grand house. I half expected the gate to shut us out, but it opened when I pushed it. The drapes were pulled across the large windows, preventing me from seeing if anyone was inside. Drawing in a deep breath, I knocked on the door. A moment passed, and my heart fluttered nervously. Maybe this was a bad idea. I'd hoped having Bethan with me might help, but one look at the house reminded me of how terrifying Mrs Dailey had been. Maybe she couldn't call Madame Grey to complain about me now the leading witch was apparently missing, but picking a fight with an older, more experienced witch who hated my family was bound to end badly no matter what I did. On the other hand, if Blythe was responsible, the town's safety depended on us undoing what she'd done. We had to risk the wrath of Mrs Dailey.

As we waited, I scanned the garden. The hedges had been cut into the shapes of various woodland animals, a surprising touch from someone as prickly as Mrs Dailey, and bright flowers adorned the beds underneath the windows. I stared, recognising the purple petals. No wonder Sky hadn't wanted to come with me. The flowers were poisonous to fairies. It was lucky I hadn't touched any of them when I'd fled the house earlier.

The door opened, and Blythe looked out. Her eyes widened at the sight of us.

"You shouldn't be here!" she said in a panicked voice. "My mum is out, but if she comes back and sees you—"

"We came to talk to you," I said. "You needed my help, remember?"

She nodded, not looking happy. "Yeah. I didn't come to your flat, because your neighbour was awful to me the last time I did."

"Oh," I said. "Yeah, she was, but you argued with her before you... changed."

Blythe blinked. "I changed?"

Bethan leaned over and whispered, "Wow. Is she being serious?"

"Apparently," I muttered. I turned to Blythe again. "Did you come into Dritch & Co's office on Saturday and see Veronica?"

She frowned. "Your work office? You mean—"

Bethan cleared her throat. "My mother spoke to you on the phone on Saturday and then you visited afterwards, didn't you?"

"No," she said. "I didn't."

Lie.

Finally, a sign that she was being less than sincere. I'd been beginning to think *I* was the one who was losing my mind.

"Blythe, you won't get into trouble if you tell us the truth," I said, trying to keep my tone gentle.

"I am," she insisted. "I don't know why everyone thinks I'm guilty. I'm the one who lost my powers. My mother is furious. She thinks the covens are plotting—" She cut herself off, looking stricken.

"The covens are plotting against you?" I glanced at Bethan, whose brows rose.

"No!" Blythe shook her head frantically. "Not at all. My mother… she's been paranoid about the covens for a long time. That's why she doesn't want you here."

Truth.

"I thought she hated me because of my family," I said. "What—never mind. Are you sure you didn't call or walk into our office on Saturday? Veronica is missing and Callie probably is by now, too."

"I didn't do anything to them!" she said, her eyes brimming over with tears. I'd never seen her cry before. "I haven't—I haven't done anything to anyone. I can't. My wand is bound, remember?"

Bethan made an *oh* noise, while I wanted to smack myself in the forehead for forgetting something so blindingly obvious. When Blythe had been fired, the coven leaders had bound her wand so she couldn't use it to harm others. While that binding might not prevent her from cursing herself, she couldn't do anything to other people. Unless she'd asked someone else to cast the hex on her behalf, but who would agree to run around hexing people on Blythe's orders? And how had she ended up getting hit? Unless it spread like a virus, but as far as I knew, magic wasn't contagious.

"But you did speak to the boss on Saturday?" asked

Bethan.

Her shoulders slumped. "I wanted my powers back. Rita couldn't help, and the council…" She faltered.

"What about the council?" I pressed.

"My mother didn't want me asking them," she said, dropping her gaze. "If they find out I have no magic—no. She won't let me do it. She'll confine me here forever."

"Your mother threatened to lock you up?" I raised an eyebrow. "Why not use your wand to get out? The binding wouldn't prevent you from doing that."

"She's better with a wand than I'll ever be," Blythe said. "And she's angry enough to use it against me if I make our family look like fools. My mind-reading talent was all I had, and hers is better."

No lies there. Bethan shifted next to me. "So you spoke to my mother to ask if she knew how to undo the curse?"

"She…" Blythe nodded. "She must have left that afternoon, because she never picked up her phone. I assumed she'd gone home—I thought it was weird that she was working on the weekend as it is."

"She's had a lot to handle," said Bethan. "And it's not that unusual for her. So she got hit by the curse at some point before the phone call… are you sure she was acting normal at the office? Someone might have cursed you and made it so that you pass it on to people you interact with."

"But I'd have caught it by now if they had," I pointed out. "And I haven't. Alissa has, and she had even less interaction with Blythe than I did."

"You don't have to talk about me like I'm not here," said Blythe, sounding more like the old Blythe than she had in a long time. "I don't know how it happened. How many people have lost their powers now?"

"I don't know," I said honestly. "Callie can still shift into a wolf, but maybe it only blocks witch powers. Or maybe there are two curses? Which do you remember taking place first?"

Blythe blinked in confusion. "Which what?"

"You said you woke up with no powers, right?" I asked. "Did you immediately feel, er, different? Like coming and talking to me?"

She shook her head. "No, I wanted to talk to Madame Grey first."

True. "But you couldn't find her… or could you?"

"She wasn't available. I—then my mother got suspicious and dragged me home. If you spend too long around me, she'll think you did it."

"I think she already does," I murmured. "Look, is there anyone you can think of who might have had a good reason to curse you?"

She gave a frantic head-shake. "I told you my wand's bound. I can't do any magic as it is. There's no point in anyone cursing me." She sniffed. "I can't even get a job interview, because most of them go through Dritch & Co."

"See, that's reason enough for her mother to come after us," Bethan muttered to me. "I'm not convinced she's in the clear."

"Do you want to speak to *her?*" I asked. "I'd honestly rather join the High Fliers. Blythe, are you sure *she* didn't do it?"

"No!" Blythe shot another panicked look behind her. "Look… my mum might be angry that I got fired, but she blames the covens more than she blames Veronica. And she wouldn't hit Callie with anything. She's terrified of werewolves."

Interesting… and not particularly helpful. "If she blames the covens, wouldn't she have reason to go after Madame Grey?"

"No. She doesn't want the town to fall apart. Why are you blaming my family?"

No lies there…

"I don't know what to believe," I admitted. "You were the first person affected, right? And unless the curse spreads like a virus, someone is going after people you've interacted with in the last few days. Except not everyone. Like me and Nina."

"Nina?" said Blythe. "*She* has good reason to do it. She hates me."

"She already told Rita she didn't," I said. "And you know I can sense lies."

Her jaw jutted out. "She's an expert liar. She managed to talk Madame Grey into letting her rent one of her houses when her mother's plotting to—" She cut herself off.

"Plotting what?" I asked.

"Nothing," Blythe mumbled.

"That didn't sound like nothing." Maybe Nina hadn't been entirely truthful after all. Madame Grey didn't rent out her houses to just anyone, though. And she'd let *me* rent a flat with Alissa when at the time, I hadn't even thought I was a real witch. Surely she wouldn't let anyone move into the house who wasn't trustworthy. Nina had said she and her mother were trying to set up their own coven, and she hadn't lied.

The door opened behind Blythe, and her younger sister stuck her head out. "What are you doing? Mum's walking up the hill—she's almost here."

Blythe jumped. "Blair. Leave, now!"

My heart jumped into my throat. I grabbed Bethan and dragged her behind one of the animal-shaped hedges, not a moment too soon. The gate opened and Blythe's mother's imperious form appeared. I held my breath, ducking low.

"Hey, Mum!" said Rebecca. I breathed out when Mrs Dailey walked past our hiding spot to the front door without glancing in our direction.

"What are you two doing?" she asked, by way of a greeting. "Close the door and get back inside."

I remained very still, as did Bethan. Blythe disappeared into the hallway, followed by Mrs Dailey. I waited a few seconds to make sure she didn't come back out, then scanned the garden for another way out. *Over the fence it is, then.*

Bethan raised an eyebrow at me as I made for the fence, but followed without arguing. The gate was in view of the door and the windows, after all.

I climbed the fence awkwardly, using my boots to propel myself above the ground, then reached to help Bethan climb up behind me. Then we more or less ran downhill, away from the house.

"That was a close one," I breathed.

"Tell me about it," said Bethan, equally breathless. "Blythe is like a stranger. But her mother must believe it's her, since she hasn't kicked her out of the house."

"I don't know what to believe," I said. "I can't trust a word this new Blythe says."

"You're telling me. But Nina... what did she mean about her mother plotting something? That might be worth looking into."

"I've never met her mum. Who is she?" I asked.

She shook her head. "No clue. Alissa would know… or you could just ask Nina herself. I mean, you do live in the same house."

"She's annoyed with me for suspecting her as it is. And I really don't think she'd have had reason to curse Veronica or Callie. Veronica's not on the council, is she?"

"No. She's more interested in running Eldritch & Co than leadership. She…" Bethan trailed off. "Veronica *has* been at council meetings more than usual the last couple of weeks, but that's because of the security issue."

"Was she for or against bringing the hunters in?" I asked. "Wait—someone hired us for that, didn't they?" *Might it have been one of the council members?*

She nodded. "Yes. We never found out who it was. I think I'm going to head back to her office and see if she left anything else lying around. Blair, you can come, but the High Fliers usually finish around four."

"Oh," I said. "Can you call me if you find anything? I don't want you falling victim to the curse, too."

"Don't worry," said Bethan. "I put on a protective spell my mum taught me. The curse won't get *me* that easily."

"If you're sure," I said. As much as I wanted answers, getting to Alissa before she pulled a disappearing act like the other victims of the curse was more important than going through Veronica's desk. Besides, Blythe wasn't hexing everyone she ran into. I hadn't been affected yet, or Bethan. Either she was covering up to gain my trust, or someone else entirely was behind this.

"I'm sure," said Bethan. "Stay out of trouble, Blair."

"I'll try to." Once I got Alissa back on the ground.

10

I broke into a fast walk, switching on the boots again. If anything, our conversation with Blythe had left us with even more questions than before. Such as which coven might have had reason to bring down our boss's business and unseat Madame Grey in one fell swoop.

Was my neighbour really involved? If it was the old Blythe making the accusation, I'd say no without hesitation, but this new Blythe was an unpredictable stranger. Honestly, anyone who wanted to vote out Madame Grey might be responsible. Anyone unscrupulous enough to ruin a bunch of innocent people's lives in the process, anyway. What didn't make sense was that they'd gone to my workplace and hit Callie and Veronica with the same curse. They didn't need to bring down Dritch & Co to take over the town's council or the covens, if that was their goal.

I was way out of my depth. The only weird thing that'd taken place at work lately was the sudden request from an unknown person to interview hunters for security, and for all I knew, it was standard procedure and Veronica would have been able to offer an explanation. Whoever had put the hunters on our call list, they'd need Madame Grey's approval to bring in outside security no matter what.

"Blair?"

Lost in thought, I'd walked right past Nathan without noticing.

"Oh," I said. "Hi."

Great job sounding enthusiastic there, Blair.

"I thought you were going home," he said.

"I was, but—the curse hit Alissa."

I quickly told him about the afternoon's events, including our talk with Blythe. Nathan might not be able to undo spells, but he had an impartial perspective that nobody else did, especially when it came to the covens. Admittedly, his only view of Blythe had come through me, and she'd tried to drive a wedge between the two of us when I'd first started at Dritch & Co, but it wouldn't hurt to have someone else aware that there might be a conspiracy to bring the covens down.

"So the curse seems to be moving of its own accord, or the caster is evading attention," he mused.

"Or it's Blythe. Obviously, it's not like I can find Callie to ask who else came into work on Saturday, assuming that's when it happened. As for Madame Grey, people walk in and out of the witches' place all the time. And Alissa… it depends on whether she was at home or in the hospital when the curse hit her. But Blythe seems determined to blame it on our new neighbour, Nina. Her natural talent blocks other magic."

"And has your neighbour shown signs of hostility towards Alissa as well?"

"Well, no," I admitted. "She said she didn't do it and my lie-sensing power didn't go off. But I'm starting to think my lie-sensing ability is a fairy power, not a witch one."

He nodded. "You know your own magic best, Blair."

Not the response I'd expected. I'd casually acknowledged my fairy weirdness, and he hadn't so much as blinked.

"Also, Callie shifted," I added, before the silence got too awkward. "So werewolf powers aren't affected. Just witch ones, I think. As I said, though, Alissa wasn't willing to stop for a chat. I was on my way to ambush her by the lake to talk some sense into her. I'm the only one of us with the keys to the flat now, not to mention her phone."

"I think it would help if you got a general idea of when exactly the curse came on," he said. "That way, you might be able to trace the person responsible without putting yourself in harm's way."

Is he worried about me? Again?

"Yeah, it would help," I said. "With Alissa… if it was at the hospital, there'll be records of everyone who came in. If they got her at home, not many people can get through our security. Madame Grey even doctored the windows so nobody can cast spells through them if they're left open." It didn't stop Sky the cat from getting in and out, but that cat was a mystery wrapped in an enigma.

"Right," said Nathan. "In the meantime, is there anyone you suspect aside from Blythe?"

"She pinned the blame on Nina, who already said she didn't do it. It would also help to know who tried to hire Veronica to bring in paranormal hunters as external security. Maybe they cursed her when she refused. Or someone else disagreed and cursed her to stop her from contacting them at all." The former was more likely, if just because she'd put the files right there on our desks, and the person who'd cursed her would surely know that someone else might make the call instead.

"I may be able to help with that," he said. "I tried to get through to Madame Grey today on the matter of the security, but she's not answering her phone and doesn't seem to be at her house either."

I groaned. "It's a mess. Only Blythe seems remotely sane, and that's because she's been replaced with her nice twin while the evil one's locked in a basement somewhere."

He raised an eyebrow. "Are you sure there isn't a replacement spell being used? Because as far as I've heard, personality-altering spells that last longer than a day or two are difficult to work. Not that I'm an expert."

"I was joking," I said wearily. "Sorry. I'm having... a week. Can you really find out who hired Dritch & Co to call the hunters? I'd call them myself, but they already think there's a werewolf on the loose as it is."

"I told the person I spoke to that the situation was under control," Nathan said. "As of yet, I don't believe they plan to send anyone in, since nobody's actually been invited."

"Nope, because Dritch & Co is imploding," I said. "But if the people who hired us decided to go directly to them..."

"Exactly," he said. "I'll make a call or two and see who might have kicked this off. I wouldn't have thought

Madame Grey would have allowed another person to act without first consulting the rest of the council."

"Vincent implied she didn't," I said. "Before she vanished."

He frowned. "The vampire knows?"

"The vampire's a mind-reader," I said. "Goes with the territory. He also refused to help, as usual, when he could easily have at least tried to speak to the other council members or covered for Madame Grey's absence."

"It's not in his interests to," he said. "It *is* in his interests to keep the hunters firmly away from his people, and the same with the werewolves."

"He doesn't exactly look out for his fellow vampires, though, does he?" I said. "Look what a fuss was necessary to get him to intervene when the werewolves nearly kicked off a war. He looked totally bored through the whole thing."

"He did? I wasn't paying attention." There was something in his tone I couldn't place. Was he jealous that I'd seen Vincent and not him? Surely not.

"Anyway—I need to go and fetch Alissa before she crashes her broom," I said. "I don't think she's even ridden one since she quit, from what she said."

"Need me to help?" he asked.

"Unless you've learned to fly, you're probably best dealing with the hunters. But I'd appreciate it if you could let me know who might have an interest in bringing in the hunters as security."

"Honestly, there's a range of opinions on the subject," he said. "I doubt I can find out what was said in a top-secret council meeting, but I can ask if they've had any calls."

"Good—more than good. Thank you. I don't know how I always end up surrounded by chaos, but I really need to find Alissa. Thanks so much." I switched my boots back on.

"Blair..."

I halted, my heart jumping. "Yes?"

He hesitated, then shook his head. "Nothing. Go and find your friend."

"Okay, I'll see you later."

I left, wondering what he'd been planning to say. At least we'd had a conversation—more than one—without coming into conflict and without me accidentally saying anything stupid or casting a spell on either of us. And I'd added in a casual mention of my fairy status and he hadn't even commented. Like it was normal. Maybe there was hope left for us after all, assuming I managed to rescue Alissa and get Madame Grey back before the hunters swarmed all over the town arresting people.

Maybe another coven *did* want to unseat Madame Grey and had cursed her in order to make the job easy. Perhaps the same people had taken down Veronica. But I'd thought anyone who wanted to take Madame Grey's place had also wanted to bring in the paranormal hunters. Why would they then curse Veronica? Because she wouldn't do it? With both of them missing and no clear suspects, it was anyone's guess.

I wove down a side street, in the direction of the lake. The path uphill, towards the waterfall, remained peaceful and deserted, unlike a few weeks ago when there'd been gargoyles swarming everywhere. Maybe if I got a moment's peace, I might even be able to go to the falls again.

The High Fliers had dispersed along the lake's edge. Some of them had gathered in groups to talk, but most were leaving, heading back into the town. I scanned the group and spotted Alissa walking away with her broom balanced on her shoulder. I followed, and she stopped, turning to scowl at me.

"Didn't I tell you to leave me alone?" she snapped.

I reached into my bag. "I just wanted to tell you I have your phone and keys. You left them at home. Where are you going?"

"None of your business." She sped up as I reached her side, shifting her grip on the broom. "What would it take for you to leave me alone?"

"Honestly? My best friend back. I know she's in there somewhere."

Alissa snorted and flipped the broom over. Oh no. Was she going to jump on her broomstick here and now?

Her leg swung over the broom and she kicked off the ground. In a whirl of air that nearly knocked me flat on my back, she shot into the air.

"Alissa!"

I lost my head, jumping to grab the broom and tug it back to earth. Alissa leaned forwards on the end, causing the broom to pitch forwards, dragging me along like a boat pulling a jet-skier.

"You can't fly off now!" I yelped, my feet skidding in the mud.

"Don't tell me what I can't do!"

Alarmed, I clicked on my levitating boots, but in doing so, I lost my grip on gravity. The broom lurched up, pulling me along with it. Whatever spell caused it to rise into the air was stronger than my ability to pull it back down to earth.

"Alissa! Stop!"

Too late. The broom yanked me into the air, and I lurched wildly along with the bucking broomstick as Alissa skirted the lake's edge. Several people pointed and laughed at us. I waved frantically at them. "Help me stop her! She's going to ride off and do something stupid."

Nobody intervened. Even the merpeople in the shallows of the lake pointed and laughed as Alissa's broom dipped and my feet skated the water. Then the broom rose higher again, making my head spin. The water swirled below, reminding me of one of my flying dreams but with infinitely less coordination involved. It was a good job I didn't get airsick.

"Alissa!" I yelped as she rocked the broom forwards in an apparent attempt to throw me off. Oh, no. *I am not going to fall into the lake wrestling my cursed best friend off a broomstick.*

"Let go!" she yelled, giving the broom a last firm tug. My grip broke and I fell. Thanks to the boots, I didn't tumble into the lake, but hung upside-down in mid-air, gasping for breath. Alissa about-turned and flew north towards the forest.

I flipped the right way up, dragging my head through the water in the process, and shoved a handful of wet hair out of my eyes. With a kick, I flew up to Alissa's level again.

"You're not going into the woods like that! You'll crash." Or end up on shifter or elf territory, which would be a whole other disaster.

I lunged for the end of her broom, narrowly missing colliding with a tree when she swung wildly to the left.

"What are you thinking?" she yelled.

"You're the one who's not thinking!" I tried to pull her down gently with me, but she clung onto the broomstick and flew higher, causing branches to scrape against my head. If she kept flying at this height, I'd take an oak tree to the face and possibly crash-land in the elf king's home. But if I let go, she might fly out of town. Then I'd never be able to help her undo the curse.

Taking a wild swing for my pocket with my free hand, I pulled out my wand and pointed it at the broom. There was no time to be careful. I cast a spell, which missed and hit a tree. My second spell caused the broom to levitate higher instead of landing. At least we'd missed the trees—but we kept flying, higher and higher. Alissa yelped, trying to get control over the broomstick, but the spell kept it rising higher despite her attempts to land.

"What have you done, idiot?" she yelled.

"I'm trying to help!" With another wave of my wand, I tried to reverse the spell, but a jet of water shot from my wand instead, drenching both of us. Another wave caused a tree to catch on fire. What would people below think was happening?

"Leave the woods, Alissa, please!" I yelped, as the broom spiralled over the forest again. Nobody in the woods would see us, since the trees were large and sprawling and blocked out most natural light, but if we crashed, we'd be lucky to come out in one piece.

I reversed the levitation spell and the broom lurched down, back under Alissa's control again. She adjusted her grip and turned north, back towards the lake.

"Not again!"

And now we were back over the water, the golden lake spinning below. The bobbing heads of merpeople and nereids popped up and down in the water, their hands waving and pointing at us. Even the remaining High Fliers on the bank cheered and whistled.

Oh no. They'd probably put 'casting spells while clinging to the end of someone else's broomstick' on their list for their next performance.

Panting, I pulled myself upright, took aim, and fired off a de-spelling charm at the end of Alissa's broom.

Abruptly, the broomstick dropped like a stone. Alissa let out a startled scream, legs flailing as the broom began falling rapidly. I grabbed the broom to steady her, but the force of her descent was too much for my levitating boots. I held on with both hands, desperately, and my wand slipped from my grasp, tumbling into the water below.

No!

I waved my left hand wildly, on the off chance of conjuring up some of the magic I'd once used without a wand before—but nothing happened.

The water glittered like a mirror. The wind rushed past, whipping back my hair. My grip broke, and I flailed both hands. *Stop. I can fly. I can!*

Something *clicked,* and I felt wings unfurl behind my shoulders. The wind caught my wings, carrying both of us into more of a swoop than a plummet. Alissa's screaming turned to a cry of delight, and the next second, we were tumbling head over heels onto the bank.

I gasped for breath, sprawled in a heap—but alive and unhurt. Alissa half lay across her broomstick, wearing a slightly dazed expression. Slowly, she rolled off the broom and lay on her back, breathless. Then she looked sideways at me. "Blair…"

Did I undo the spell? I'd de-glamoured, again, and was in full fairy guise, wings and all. I also didn't know how to switch the glamour on again, but I was too relieved to do anything but breathe.

"Hey, Alissa," I said, with an attempt at a smile. She might have nearly drowned us, but it wasn't really her fault.

"You're shedding glitter, Blair," she said, and cracked up laughing as though she'd told a hilarious joke.

I looked down at myself. My hands glowed faintly green, and glitter sprinkled my soaking wet clothes.

Someone nudged my foot and I started upright, but it was one of the merpeople. He held out my wand. "Oh, my god, thank you!" I thought I recognised him—he was one of the merpeople who Alissa and I had helped by getting rid of a particularly annoying pirate vampire ghost a few weeks ago. "Thanks so much."

Alissa rose to her feet, picking up her broomstick.

"Hang on," I said quickly. "You're not—"

She shot me an angry glare. "I might not be able to ride my broom, but I'll come home with you when hell freezes over."

"No chance." I raised my wand, and cast a binding spell on her, grabbing her wrist as I did so. She yelped and tried to run, but I'd cuffed us together. Silently thanking Rita for teaching me that one, I pulled her firmly to my side.

"Let go of me!" she yelped.

"Nope," I said. "We're going to see the witches."

11

I managed to drag Alissa back to the coven headquarters despite her furious protests and frequent attempts to escape my grasp. I hadn't turned my glamour back on but was too occupied trying to keep hold of Alissa to notice the stares this time around. It was lucky being in fairy form hadn't shrunk me to pixie size, because Alissa took every opportunity to try to pull out of my grip, and wrestling her through the doors of the coven headquarters was like putting clothes on an octopus.

Rita took one look at us and waved her wand. The water and dirt vanished from our clothes, while Alissa's broom zipped out of her hand and levitated to the desk.

"That broom is coven property," she said. "What are you two doing?"

"Let me go!" Alissa yelled, squirming against my grip.

"She's under the curse," I explained. "She tried to fly off, and… things got out of hand. We crash-landed by the lake. She's mad at me now but she'll thank me for this when she comes to her senses. Is there a way to secure her in the flat so she can't run off?"

Rita blinked. "One thing at a time. I'll take the broom… it's de-spelled. Who did that?"

"I did," I said.

She gave me another disbelieving brink. "You de-spelled the broom while *riding it?*"

I flushed. "Not really. I used my boots to catch up to her at first, then I had to take off the glamour to stop us from crashing." I gestured to my wings and shed glitter in the process. In fact, I'd left a trail of pink and purple sprinkles all over the lobby. "Sorry, I don't know how to make that stop."

"Never mind, Blair," she said, a touch of weariness in her voice. "What happened to Alissa?"

"She's a madwoman and a spoilsport!" Alissa said.

"She tried to join the High Fliers and nearly crashed into the lake," I supplied. "I couldn't find Madame Grey and I was worried she'd hurt herself. Can you—"

Rita waved her wand and Alissa let out a startled squeak as a chair shifted into position behind her, causing her to fall into it. She tried to stand, but her legs locked into place.

"I can't stand up!" she protested.

"It's a temporary precaution," said Rita.

Alissa squirmed. "You're holding me against my will!"

Rita gave her a stern look. "You broke the law in stealing that broomstick. I'm required to hold you here for questioning."

"I thought the broom was hers," I said. "Er, since she used to be part of the High Fliers."

"No, I gathered she sold her old broom when she quit," Rita said. "What is this spell she's under?"

"Same curse as before," I responded. "Like Blythe, but the opposite. Rather than turning nice and docile, she's being mean and reckless."

"And you're a boring—"

Rita pointed her wand and cast a silencing spell. Alissa's mouth opened and closed, and she fell back in the seat, her expression murderous. With a silent yell, she yanked the chair forwards, nearly tipping off it. Rita waved her wand again, and Alissa flopped back, her eyes closed.

"I'll have to wake her up to question her," she said. "So we can find out who did this. How did it start?"

"I don't know when it hit her," I said. "She was really grumpy yesterday. Then she woke up and grabbed a broomstick instead of going to work, and here we are."

Rita looked perturbed. "How many victims now?"

"Blythe, Callie, my boss, and now Alissa. And—her grandmother's missing," I added.

Rita's breath escaped in a sigh. "I know. I've been covering for her all day. She disappeared yesterday, sometime after the meeting."

Oh, no. It's true. Some part of me had been hanging on, against the admittedly slim odds, to the possibility that Madame Grey was occupied in some other way. Not cursed. *This is bad. Really bad.*

"She was definitely in a meeting yesterday?" My heart began to beat louder. "With the coven leaders? Who?"

"A private meeting with all the coven heads," she said. "But since then, she's been absent."

"So is my boss," I said. "Bethan told me she probably

left town to look for her ex-husband. Meanwhile, Callie lost her temper and shifted into a wolf to run away, so her family will probably come gunning for me next—assuming the hunters who heard her growling on the phone don't get here first."

I sank into a seat beside Alissa's unconscious form, only remembering my fairy wings when they brushed uncomfortably against the back of the chair.

"Blair, calm down," Rita said, though she looked fairly stressed herself. "I can't say I've seen Veronica, I'm sorry. Or Blythe."

"I saw Blythe earlier,' I said. "I went to question her with Bethan—Veronica's daughter. She claims innocence and blamed it on my neighbour again. Do you know which coven Nina belongs to? Wait, she said she's starting a new one with her mother."

"They used to belong to the Nightshade Coven," Rita told me. "Her mother was at the meeting."

"And the other coven leaders?" I asked. "Were they affected?"

"I'll speak to them, but as far as I know, none of them is unaccounted for like Madame Grey. She was meant to be meeting with the vampires this evening, but clearly, that isn't going to be possible."

That would tick Vincent off. "The vampires' leader might know, but he's refusing to get involved, as usual."

Her brow furrowed. "Bringing the other paranormal leaders into it will only cause more trouble—things will be dire enough if the other witches find out she's missing."

"So they don't know," I muttered. "Would any of them have reason to want to take her place so badly that they'd hex or curse her granddaughter?"

She shook her head. "There might be rivalries, but everyone respects Madame Grey. Besides, there's certainly no reason for anyone among the coven leaders to have targeted your place of employment as well. As for Alissa, she's not involved with the council at all."

"No, but maybe she got in the way by accident." I was grasping at straws now. "And… Blythe. As for Veronica, she's the person to hire if you want to bring in external security. Isn't that what the meeting was about?"

"Among other things," she said. "The covens have yet to come to an agreement, but the other paranormal leaders, especially the vampires and the werewolves, will never agree to bring in the hunters."

"That implies someone from one of the covens called the hunters, right?" I asked.

"Called them?" she echoed. "When?"

"Someone hired Dritch & Co to contact them," I said. "Nobody knows who, because Veronica disappeared. But maybe they cursed her because she refused. This is all security-related, right? They got Callie, too, and now the hunters think there are wild werewolves running amok in town because she shifted in the middle of talking to them on the phone."

"Blair, to be frank, I'm having enough trouble keeping the coven leaders from finding out Madame Grey is missing. There's supposed to be a meeting of all the paranormal group leaders tomorrow, and I'm expecting there to be a heavy debate about security again, before a vote takes place on whether to bring outsiders in or not."

"Maybe that's what someone wanted to sabotage," I said. "When do you vote?"

"Madame Grey was supposed to set the date," said Rita. "But it'll be soon."

"Did someone else act first and contact the hunters and Dritch & Co?" I said. "Did they do that behind the coven's backs?"

"Perhaps," said Rita. "I didn't ask, but Madame Grey wouldn't have done so herself. She's the one who interviews everyone new in town, and besides, our most popular idea was to simply expand the security team and hire from among the paranormals in the neighbouring village."

"Is there anyone who seems overly keen to bring in the hunters?" I asked.

"Certainly not," she said. "We just *stopped* an outright conflict between the vampires and the werewolves, and both would object to people who've hunted their fellow paranormals being allowed to relocate to the town for the purpose of policing us. I gather that Nathan was subject to a fairly extensive interview process when he came here."

"I guess that makes sense. Right now he's handling the hunters and trying to find out who called them. But I don't know if it's connected to..." I waved a hand at Alissa. "It seems like someone's trying to destabilise the covens."

"It may be that Madame Grey had a good reason to leave and she'll be back tomorrow morning as promised," said Rita. "She's had a rather trying few weeks, and I don't blame her for wanting to get away."

"But she wouldn't leave when something important was going on," I said. And Alissa wouldn't abandon her responsibilities to become a broomstick stunt artist. Some things just didn't happen. "Rita, what would it take to get invited into tomorrow's meeting?"

"It's coven leaders only," she said. "You're an honorary member of the Meadowsweet Coven, but in order to try for a position on the council, you'd also need to be a qualified witch as well as frequently attending weekly meetings. While you certainly have more raw talent than we anticipated, you've yet to pass any of the higher qualifications necessary to take on a leadership position."

That's because my lessons keep getting interrupted. Though admittedly, I'd never actually been to a coven meeting in the limited free time I had. Now I wished I'd followed Helen's lead and got myself involved in the community. But even then, I wasn't qualified to come to tomorrow's meeting. I'd have to stay at home and hope that nobody put two and two together and realised someone had bested the most powerful witch in town.

"When's the meeting tomorrow?" I asked.

"Midday. Don't do anything foolish, Blair."

"Wouldn't dream of it."

Alissa stirred, groaning. "Where am I?"

"Alissa!" A wild surge of hope hit me. "Did the spell wear off?"

"What spell?" she said. "You tied me to a chair! Let me off."

"Alissa, calm down," said Rita. "I have a couple of questions to ask you. If you answer, I'll free you from the chair."

"You can't hold me like this!" She squirmed and kicked like a toddler throwing a public tantrum, but the spell held fast.

"Since you stole from the coven, technically, I can,"

said Rita. "And you're a danger to yourself as long as you're under the curse."

If I didn't know better, I'd say she was enjoying this. I'd known Rita had a mean streak from her witch classes, but I didn't like seeing it turned on Alissa, even if she was acting like a stranger.

"She'll let you go when you answer her questions," I said, attempting to sound soothing.

"Your grandmother is missing," said Rita. "When did you last see her?"

"She's missing?" Alissa's brow wrinkled. "I have no idea. She hasn't bothered to call or visit in over a week. Too busy with coven matters and boring town council meetings."

At least we'd got her attention. Maybe there was hope of getting through to her after all.

"There's an important meeting tomorrow which Madame Grey needs to attend, but she's gone," Rita told her. "It would help if you could tell us everyone you've seen over the last couple of days."

Good idea. Rather than insisting there was something wrong with Alissa and making her go on the defensive, I ought to have gone for a more relaxed approach and asked more questions. Admittedly, that approach wouldn't really work in the broomstick situation, but I was glad I had at least one sensible and level-headed person on my side at the moment.

Alissa squirmed in her seat. "No. I was at the hospital dealing with a screaming elf throwing a tantrum and a group of angry werebadgers. Then I came home."

"Did you see Blythe when you came home?" I asked her.

"Blythe? No. Just the neighbours."

The neighbours… "Including Nina?"

She nodded. "Yeah, she got in around the same time as I did."

Whoa. Might Blythe be right? But Nina had outright said she hadn't done it. And there didn't seem any logical reason to go after Alissa. She was a nurse, not on the council, and while it'd taken me entirely too long to even notice she might be under a curse, whoever had done this surely knew about my lie-sensing ability and that it would take one question for me to know the truth.

"On the way back from work?" I asked. "Er, did you use your healing powers at all that day?"

"Yes, I did."

So her healing ability had still been working. That implied she'd been put under the curse after leaving the hospital. Nina wouldn't be pleased to be accused again, but I couldn't think of any other way to get the right information. It was either her or Blythe, and she was the one with the ability to cancel out other witches' magic…

"What are you thinking, Blair?" asked Rita.

"That Nina seems the logical person to have done it. Except she has no motive. It just doesn't feel right."

"Perhaps the person responsible is trying to frame her," she said. "She did strike me as genuine."

"Blythe thinks Nina is framing *her*," I said, beginning to get a headache. "I don't know what issue those two have, but I think it's to do with their families."

Of the two, Blythe still seemed the most likely. If Nina and her mother had wanted to start their own coven and Madame Grey wouldn't let them, it would make sense, but Madame Grey had given Nina the flat upstairs in our house. It wouldn't make sense for Nina to pay her back by cursing her.

"Are you ever going to get me out of this chair?" Alissa wanted to know.

"Yes." I looked at Rita. "Can you help me get her back to the flat? I think it's the safest place for her, and hopefully the curse will break before she can do anything drastic like try to move out."

"Put a binding spell on the doors," said Rita. "And windows. All of them. And don't forget that she can still use a wand. The curse must switch off latent talents. You're saying Blythe definitely didn't do it?"

"Not only did she not do it, it's clearly not affecting every single person she comes into contact with," I said. "Otherwise it'd have got me, too."

"Yes, you said," she said distractedly. "I'm going to tell the others in the Meadowsweet Coven that Madame Grey is coming down with flu. Perhaps it's not the best way to handle this, but if anyone finds out she's missing, there'll be chaos. She's right in the middle of several projects which will shape the future of the town."

"And—tomorrow? What if she doesn't show up at the meeting? People will get suspicious."

"They will," she said. "But we'll deal with that tomorrow. Keep it quiet for tonight, Blair, even if you decide to go on any excursions."

I couldn't argue with that. Tomorrow was another day, another chance.

Rita raised her wand. "Are you ready for me to undo the spell on Alissa's chair?"

"Wait..." I looked down at myself. "I need to redo my

glamour. Ah, never mind, I'll do it later. Should I use another binding spell?"

"Yes, I think you should."

There wasn't anything more to do. Bethan was looking for her mother, Nathan was contacting the hunters, and I definitely didn't have good reason to gate-crash a council meeting to interrogate some of the members on the off-chance that one of them had cursed Madame Grey.

That left one solution: show up early to the meeting and talk to the coven leaders without giving away that I suspected anyone of foul play. If I showed up looking like this, though, I could forget being taken seriously. I really needed to figure out how to turn my fairy glamour off and on without needing to be in a life-or-death situation in order to use it.

Maybe I could break into Madame Grey's office on the off chance that she might have left a clue or two about where she'd wandered off to. She was important enough that she had meetings and important obligations all over the place, and keeping her absence quiet was pretty much an exercise in futility. Rita must surely know that. It wasn't like I knew any spells that would allow me to track a person down. They were far beyond my level. Besides, I needed to get Alissa safely back home before she found a way to wriggle out of Rita's trap before doing anything risky.

After binding Alissa's hand to mine once again, I towed her out of the classroom and into the lobby, shedding more glitter. *I wish I could stop that.* I *should* know how to turn my glamour off and on by now, too. The pixie had redone it the last couple of times, but I didn't know where the little creature was, and I needed to stop being dependent on it to help me.

"What are you doing?" snapped Alissa. "Aren't you supposed to be taking me to jail?"

"We're going home," I answered, irritation suddenly rising. I didn't blame Alissa, but I was too tired to be yelled at again. "I'm trying to turn off these wings so people don't stare."

"Who cares?"

Who cared indeed? I had bigger problems. Sighing, I steered Alissa out of the coven headquarters and down the street. It was awkward walking with my left hand bound to hers, let alone with wings making my balance lopsided. When she tried to yank me off my feet, I fluttered my wings and left the ground, finding it easier to float and pull Alissa after me rather than stumbling along. My right hand was free, but I couldn't cast spells with it, so I had to rely on the binding to keep her from running off. I kept floating, wishing I'd kept my left hand free instead. People stared at both of us—a lopsided fairy dragging an angry witch along. What a mess. You'd think I'd be able to re-glamour, considering I was the one who'd undone the glamour to begin with…

I frowned at my glittering right hand as we reached the front doors. Wait. I'd been flailing madly around under a broomstick at the time, but—witch magic worked best in my left hand. Was that because my fairy powers worked best in my right one? I'd definitely waved my right hand around while I'd been up in the air.

I snapped the fingers of my right hand. Glitter swirled around me, blown away on the breeze—and my feet touched the floor.

Yes! I'd done it. My wings were gone, my fairy form hidden away, and this time, I hadn't needed the pixie's help.

Now all I needed to do was wrangle Alissa into the flat and put boundary spells everywhere. The other coven leaders would be here tomorrow at noon, which gave me... not enough time to find Madame Grey. Not to mention figure out who might have wanted her out of the picture. If they wanted to take her place, why block the powers of other witches, let alone mess with their personalities? I dreaded to think what sort of a state Madame Grey might be in, but if Alissa was any indication, she was probably zipping over the rooftops on another stolen broom.

One way to find out. As soon as I got Alissa sorted, I'd look up how to use a tracking spell.

12

Alissa was *not* pleased to be confined. I had to walk around the flat with her chained to my hand—switching the binding spell from my left to my right hand so my left hand was free to use my wand—and set up boundaries around every room. Now she couldn't set foot outside the flat. She also couldn't harm me, because I'd confiscated her wand and hidden it away. I'd thought losing the leader of the town was bad, but after an hour, I'd have given almost anything for Alissa to be the first to get cured. She was downright unbearable, snapping at the slightest noise, slamming the windows as though she hoped to break the spell trapping her inside by sheer force, and storming around, terrifying Roald. I ended up inviting both cats to hang out in my room while Alissa got her tantrum over with. Every attempt to start a conversation was met with huffiness, and in the end, she stormed into her own room to sulk.

I took the chance to sneak into the living room to the

bookshelf where she kept all her textbooks. Roald followed, looking despondent.

"Sorry," I whispered, stroking him behind the ears. "You'll have your witch back before you know it, mark my words."

I snagged Alissa's advanced spellbook from the shelf, brought it into my room, and got to work looking up a tracking spell. It might be that Rita or someone else—like Madame Grey's own family, for instance—had already tried tracking her down that way, but I was all out of ideas.

"Two *days?*" I scanned the relevant page in the textbook. "It takes two days to brew? That's too long."

"Miaow," said Sky, sprawling on the bed next to me.

Roald just blinked dejectedly, curled on my other side. I stroked him, sighing inwardly. Two days. Far too late for the council meeting... but what else could I do? I ran a finger down the list of ingredients. It was definitely doable, but I'd need to 'borrow' a few things from the witches' stores.

Sky yawned and stretched, and I stroked him. "Sky, hypothetically, could you break into the witches' ingredient stores?"

He gave me a look that said, *of course.*

"I'm going to need your help," I said to him. "As you can see, Alissa isn't herself. Her grandmother is missing, and I've never used a tracking spell before. I don't have the right ingredients here. Would you be able to get them for me?"

I expected him to lie down and say no in cat-speak, or just take off. But he blinked his oddly coloured eyes and jumped off the bed. *Was that a yes?* You could never tell with cats. He might be thinking of hunting mice instead. And logically, there wasn't any real reason I couldn't go myself. Leaving Alissa, though… unless I bound her to her room, that wasn't happening.

Sky batted the bedroom door with a paw. Why he wanted *me* to let him out when he could walk through walls, I'd probably never know. I obliged and let Sky out of the flat, my spirits rising a little. The cat was on my side. And if I got to Madame Grey, and persuaded her to come back so we could take the curse off her… okay, I hadn't got that far yet. But it was a start.

Two days to brew the tracking spell. Could the covens survive that long without a leader? Rita must surely have a backup plan, but without knowing *where* Madame Grey was, there was no way to prove she was under a curse, much less that someone had put it on her on purpose. I very nearly gave in and called Alissa's family again, but if I did, everyone would find out their leader was missing. Rita had insisted I didn't tell anyone, for tonight at least. She probably did have a plan, one that didn't involve me. I wasn't a real coven witch, after all…

I caught sight of my reflection in the window, pale and sprinkled with glitter. After all this time, I'd still never actually seen my reflection as a fairy. Alissa had just said I was shinier than usual when I'd first come out from under the waterfall, but I'd still worried that there was a monster lurking under there. The way the others had stared at me when I'd come out of the wizard's house looking like a fairy suggested that might be the case, but maybe it was the cat who'd freaked them out. Rita hadn't blinked at holding an extended conversation with me in my fairy guise, after all.

Okay. Let's try this.

First, I locked the bathroom door so Alissa wouldn't see what I was up to. Then I took in a deep breath and faced the mirror. I held up my right hand and reached for the *spark* I'd felt when my human disguise had slipped away and left whoever I was underneath. My fingers caught the spark, snapped, and glitter flitted through the air.

When it'd disappeared, a stranger looked back at me. Big dark eyes. Pointed ears under hair that looked a few shades lighter than it normally did. My clothes felt oddly tight at the back, and the tips of wings pointed upwards. No wonder my flight had been so awkward. I'd need to either cut wing-holes into all my T-shirts or wear something that left enough breathing room to extend my wings.

My fairy form wasn't as grotesque as I'd feared. I'd had weeks of nightmares of looking into the mirror or the lake and seeing a green swamp monster staring back, but this Blair was… fine. Close enough to the human me not to make me scream in terror. I shook my head and felt the tips of my pointed ears brush against my hair. Of course I looked like me—everyone had known who I was when they'd seen me come out of the house. I'd just assumed they were all terrified. Well, the small children running away from me might have been. But this… was fine. I could learn to live with it.

I snapped the fingers of my right hand again, and the glamour snapped back into place. Fairy. Witch. Fairy witch. Both. Either. Smiling at my fairy reflection, I snapped the glamour back on and skipped out into the living room.

The pixie hovered above the sofa, wings fluttering. "Hey," I said. "Come to help me brew up a tracking spell to find Madame Grey? Or is there a fairy method that I don't know about yet?"

The pixie fluttered around, glitter spilling from its hands. Why fairies shed glitter, I had no clue, but I'd left a trail all over the witches' lobby and completely forgotten to clean it up. Not to mention Rita's classroom. She seemed too distracted to have noticed, though. The important thing was that fairy magic worked for me. Now to see if I could upgrade my witchy talents in time to save my best friend.

As minutes passed and Sky didn't return, I grew concerned. The silence from Alissa's room was concerning, too, but I could hear her breathing through the door. She must have crashed from exhaustion after riding her broom all afternoon. The pixie kept fluttering around, offering no help.

"I don't suppose you know where I can find some of the plant called pixie dust?" I asked him. "Not that it's a priority, but the elf king will probably send one of his people to collect me again at some point, and I'll have to yell at him about pixie dust being extinct."

The pixie turned to me, wings fluttering, and made a gesture I couldn't read.

"No clue what that means, sorry."

The pixie flew into my room, then landed on the open textbook. Frowning, I reached to pick it up. The pixie flew around my head, prodding the back of the book. The glossary?

Oh. Pixie dust. "It's still extinct," I said.

Wait… if it was listed at all, maybe there was still a way to find out if it still existed in any form. I skimmed to the relevant section, eagerly reading every word. Nope, still extinct. The elf king's quest was impossible, that was the point…

My bedroom door opened at the pixie's touch and it flew into the living room. I followed, pausing in front of the bookshelves. "You think there's something else there?"

I scanned the titles, and my gaze snagged on a volume that hadn't been there before: the textbook on fairies I'd once seen at the bookshop. Alissa had bought the only copy? It didn't seem like her not to tell me about it, but I picked the book up regardless. I'd have time to read it in detail later.

I skipped to the glossary. Sure enough, pixie dust was listed as an important plant for fairies… and while it was extinct, it was rumoured to grow in wet, rocky areas. Like…

The waterfall. Where else would it be? *Maybe I have a chance of finding it after all.*

I put the textbook down, suddenly buzzing with energy. I was too restless to stay confined and there was nothing I could do for anyone until Sky came back with the ingredients. And I'd been wanting to go back to the waterfall again for what felt like forever. Maybe I shouldn't be prioritising running around on the elf king's orders with my human life imploding, but I had to do *something.* Sky was out, and Alissa couldn't escape the boundaries I'd put on the flat. If I flew, I could be back within half an hour.

Putting the textbook down, I debated leaving Sky a note, then wondered if I hadn't got hit with the stupid curse after all. Cats couldn't read, even magical ones. Instead, I left the book open on the page showing the pixie dust, figuring that was enough of an explanation in itself. If not, thanks to my wings, I'd be back in a heartbeat, or wingbeat.

I grabbed my bag, left my coat behind so my wings would have room to breathe, and made for the door. Roald gave a concerned whine, and I crouched down to pet him. "Don't worry. I'm going to fix this as soon as I get back."

I bounded out of the flat, locked the door, and jumped when Nina appeared behind me.

"Oh!" I said. "Er, hey, Nina."

"What are you doing?" she asked. "I heard this awful racket coming from your flat."

"Alissa," I said. "She got hit by the same curse as Blythe, but it turned her mean. I had to stop her crashing into the lake on a broomstick."

Her face paled. "Really? I—I'm sorry."

"It's not your fault." *Is it?* "Pretty annoying, though. She's lost her mind. I suppose the only way to undo it is to catch the culprit, and it sounds like it hit her somewhere between her leaving the hospital yesterday and getting home. Did you see anyone else near the house?"

Her concerned expression didn't waver. "No, I didn't. I hope they find who did it. Unless—has Blythe been around? Have you seen her?"

"I have," I admitted. "Not here, though, and she hasn't

spoken to Alissa, as far as I know. Besides, my lie-sensing power told me she's being honest. For what it's worth. I never liked her either. She made my life a nightmare when I moved here."

She chewed on her lip. "Yeah. We went to school together. She never got any less mean after leaving. More, if anything. Is there anything I can do to help you?"

Maybe she wasn't guilty, and I was letting Blythe's words get into my head. I wasn't exactly amazing at reading people and I'd been wrong so many times lately that my faith in my own ingenuity was in doubt. But I'd figure it out later when I got hold of Madame Grey. For now, I had a quest to resolve.

"No, but I'll let you know if I do. Thanks."

I left the building, feeling more confused than ever. Our flat was protected enough that nobody could get in and Roald was there keeping watch, but leaving didn't feel right, especially when Nina may or may not be hiding a secret. But even if Alissa managed to get past the boundaries, it wasn't like she could actually do anything other than steal her broomstick back, and I trusted Rita to keep it securely away.

If the person behind the curse had wanted to distract me from my quest to find the pixie dust, they were doing a spectacular job. If not for the deadline, I wouldn't have decided to go looking for it tonight. But there wasn't anything more to do for Alissa, and if I got the elf king's quest done, I'd be able to tick one thing off my to-do list. Besides, after turning my glamour off… I wouldn't lie, I wanted to see the falls again, for the first time since before the meeting on the solstice I'd been forced to skip. I wanted to see them as a fairy.

My pace quickened as I grew more confident I wouldn't be followed, and I snapped my fingers, letting my human disguise melt away. I grinned as I flew above the town, wings spread wide, hair standing on end, and the feeling I'd felt in my dreams surging within me. Why had those dreams always turned to nightmares? There was nothing better than this, and I had to admit I understood Alissa's love of flying after all. Wheeling in the air, I descended to land on the path leading to the falls. It wasn't quite dark yet, but so quiet, even the usual sounds of chattering merpeople in the lake were dimmed. The forest bordered me on my left, the lake glittered on my right, and—I wasn't alone here.

I froze. Human voices drifted on the breeze from the forest path, close, clipped, and male. Something about their tone made my skin crawl. I ducked behind the nearest tree. Not my smartest move, but when three people appeared on the path, I was glad I hadn't taken to the skies.

The three men wore clothes that wouldn't look out of place in a hiking club, and thick coats which looked downright uncomfortable on a relatively warm summer evening. They were also human. Really human. I'd have guessed they were even if my paranormal-sensing power hadn't shown me images of them as aggressive... and dangerous.

My throat went dry, and I held very still.

"Is this the town's boundary?" asked the guy on the left, a stocky man with a slightly confused expression.

"We're *in* the town," said the central guy, who wore a scowl as though he thought the whole universe offended him. "This forest is technically owned by whoever runs the town."

"We just walked in here," mused the third guy, who was tall and thin and tired-looking. "Doesn't say much for their security. Looks like they were right to be concerned."

"We'll take care of that," said the central guy. "Just as soon as we find someone to speak to. Not one of their hairy neighbours either."

I felt sick. They were *hunters...* and it didn't sound like they were here for legal reasons. I'd thought nobody would be able to get in from outside the town. It was fixed so that no normals could even find it on a map. Right?

I remained still, my body shaking, and acutely conscious of my fairy wings and obvious non-human appearance. If I crept up on them, I might be able to waylay them before they reached the houses, but I remembered Nathan saying he had ways of telling whether someone paranormal was around even if they were invisible. And the trees were entirely too thin in this part of the woods. The hunters were armed and trained to shoot on sight, if rumour was to be believed.

"Why're there so many trees?" asked the dopey-looking man on the left.

"Because it's a forest," said the scowling guy in the centre. "Nasty place. Too many bugs."

"One bit me," said the sleepy-looking dude on the right.

"It got me, too," said the central guy. "Get out of here!" He waved his fists in the air.

I spotted the pixie floating above them, unseen, and grinned, unable to help myself. I hoped the little creature stayed out of reach, but it was worth the entertainment of seeing the three hulking idiots spin around, scratching their arms and trying to find what'd bitten them. They weren't the brightest bulbs, apparently. No wonder Nathan had quit working with them. In my head, I nicknamed them Dopey, Grumpy, and Sleepy. Now they seemed considerably less threatening. They were seriously barking up the wrong tree by walking in here to begin with.

To my relief, the three hunters turned away from my hiding spot and ambled down another path, still swatting at invisible insects.

"She's supposed to meet us here," grumbled Grumpy. "Out of sight of the lake. What's that way?"

Sleepy shifted to point diagonally across where I was hiding. "That way? Fairy Falls. Like the town name."

"Cute." He snorted. "Sounds like a lie. They need our help."

"No, we don't."

Nathan's voice was clear. I shrank into the bushes, my heart thundering so loudly I was almost certain they heard me—but their eyes were on Nathan. He walked out in front of them, and I wondered how long he'd been there. If he'd come up the path, he'd have seen me—as a fairy, no less—yet he didn't give so much as a glance in my direction.

"I don't remember any of you having permission to cross the town's boundaries," he said. "I recall telling you not to bother sending any of your people because we have it covered ourselves, actually."

"Then how were we able to stride right in?" asked Grumpy.

Good question. "Clearly, someone let you in," he said. "Someone who invited you here."

"Not one of your rabid monsters? I thought you knew better than to run with the wolves, Nathan," said Sleepy.

"This is not the place for a chat. Leave the forest and the town before you're arrested for trespassing."

"You can't arrest all three of us," said Grumpy. "They said the covens wouldn't interfere. And if the shifter animals attack us, we have permission to shoot and kill without asking questions."

"Who said the covens wouldn't interfere?" asked Nathan.

My breath caught. Someone had brought them here, and had made sure Madame Grey would be out of commission. They must have taken out the border guards in some way, too. It wasn't possible to just stride into the town, otherwise wayward normals would wander in. Okay, I'd done exactly that when I'd first come to the town, but I was paranormal. These guys were most definitely *not.*

"Nobody," answered Dopey.

Nathan stepped towards him. "Don't be a fool. You're outnumbered, trespassing in a peaceful place with hostile intentions. If someone told you that you could freely walk into the forest, they were wrong. Who told you?"

"Nobody," repeated Dopey, though he looked uncomfortable, and I didn't need my lie-sensing power to know he was lying through his teeth. I was also pretty sure that the three idiots and Nathan had a history.

I desperately needed to turn my human disguise back on before I exposed my fairy self to the same people who'd arrested my family, but if I moved, they'd see me.

I held my breath as one of the men turned sharply in my direction. "There's someone watching us in the trees."

Nope. Don't look at me. If I moved to cast a spell, I'd only alert their attention, and for all I knew, they could even see through glamour. If I ran, they might try to shoot at me. Who knew what weapons they might be hiding under those thick coats?

They moved closer, and I snapped my fingers, feeling my glamour click back into place. It wasn't hard to fake fear, because most of it was real. "What are you doing?" I yelped. "Can't a witch take an evening stroll in peace without being set upon by a bunch of Neanderthals?"

"Blair?" Nathan stared in apparent disbelief. Maybe he hadn't seen me after all.

"Who are these people?" I looked between them. "They're *normals*, aren't they? Normals aren't allowed in here."

"We are most certainly not normals!" objected Sleepy.

"No, you wouldn't be, wearing those coats in this weather," I said, unable to resist messing with them. They might have some outright prejudiced views, but they weren't the sharpest knives, and none of them seemed to know just how lucky they'd been that they hadn't run into any werewolves in the forest.

In fact, it seemed almost too convenient. Had the person who'd brought them here cleared the path so they'd be able to get to their meeting place without encountering anyone else at all?

The hunters seemed at a loss as to how to respond. "We're here on important business," said Grumpy.

I could picture him saying "I demand to speak to the manager" in the same tone at my old job.

"Then you won't mind telling us what it is. Like he said." I jerked my head at Nathan, who still looked utterly perplexed at my sudden appearance. It wasn't like this was the first time he'd run into me in the woods.

"I don't think so," said Dopey. "We're running late."

"Too bad," Nathan said. "You're not allowed in, and whatever went wrong with security won't happen again. There ought to be someone watching the border, and if I find out you deliberately sabotaged our security, with or without the help of someone within the town, you'll land on the police chief's watch list yourselves."

"And he's a gargoyle," I put in. "All of them are, in fact. Surprised they're not watching the skies."

They usually were. That alone was weird. *Who's working against us?* Why had they wanted to risk bringing hunters here, right into the woods?

Maybe I wasn't doing a great job feigning ignorance, but I was past caring. These people had marched right into the town intending to make trouble, and I wasn't having any of it.

"Yes," Nathan said. "They should be. I'll speak to the police myself."

"There's no need for that," Grumpy objected. "You need to stay out of our business."

"What happens in this town *is* my business," he said evenly.

"Clearly, it's safe enough for a young witch to walk alone in the woods," I added.

"Not unless the witch in question is a foolish one," said Grumpy.

"Not as foolish as trespassing in the woods when you don't belong here," I retaliated. "You hired someone using magic to mess with our security? Or did you bribe someone?" I looked at Dopey, who blinked stupidly.

"Uh, no, we didn't bribe anyone," he said.

True. He might sound like a fool, but someone must have intentionally let them in. Someone from the town itself.

"I'll *escort* you to the border," Nathan said firmly. "Blair, I'd advise you to go home."

"Oh, no," I said. "There's one of you and three of them. What if they jump you when your back's turned?"

"They won't." Nathan looked a little frustrated, but it mostly seemed to be directed at the outsiders. Maybe I hadn't royally screwed all this up after all. They couldn't point their fingers at me. I'd only been walking in the woods, as far as they knew.

"What are you accusing us of?" demanded Grumpy.

"Trying to disrupt the peace," I retaliated, all pretence forgotten. "You're not welcome here. And if I find out you sabotaged our security in any way, I'll see to it that you're hauled in for questioning."

I used my best 'Okay, I'll *get* the manager' voice, honed from years of throwing drunks out of the pub and expelling shoplifters. Two of the three actually backed up a bit.

"You heard her," said Nathan. "I'll call the police to inform them of your presence. I'd advise you not to take any detours, if you know what's good for you. Some won't be as kind to you for trespassing as we've been."

They backed up further. Grumpy still wore a furious expression like he wanted to start a fight, but the others knew when they were beaten. None of them could outrun a gargoyle, and if they tried to hide in the woods, it wouldn't be long before they ran into the werewolves or the elves. The gargoyles might not be the most competent, especially their chief, Steve, but they'd stepped up lately when we'd been under attack from the wizard's monster pet in the forest.

As the three hunters retreated, Nathan hesitated. I knew he wanted to follow them, but he needed to call the police. On the other hand, they'd have to pass right through shifter territory to get out of the woods either way, and if they ran into anyone, it could easily erupt into an all-out conflict. They weren't bright and had it in for 'monsters'—a recipe for trouble.

"Go after them," I said. "I'll come too."

"Not a good idea," he said. "I'm going to call Steve's people, then follow them on foot. I can direct them back onto the right track if they wander off the path."

"Okay." I didn't like sending him after them alone, but it was better than the alternative. "I'll go home. Thanks for standing up to them."

He looked me over. I held my breath, suddenly conscious that we were alone together. "Blair, you're covered in glitter."

"Oh." I flushed to my hairline. "They were meant to meet someone here, right? Shouldn't one of us stay and ambush the person who lured them in here? Maybe *they* took out the security."

"Good point." He looked sideways at me. "You'll call the police, won't you? If you find them. Don't try to confront anyone alone."

I wouldn't count on it. Poor Rita was the only authority figure I knew who might actually be inclined to lend a hand. "Sure," I lied. "I won't put myself in danger, don't worry."

"Let me know if you need help," we both said at more or less the same time. I laughed nervously. He gave me a smile in return, which I hadn't expected, and followed the hunters' path.

I turned away, hoping I could handle what was ahead.

13

I returned to the bushes to keep an eye on the path, half wishing I'd gone with Nathan. But the hunters had said they were supposed to be meeting the person who'd called them into town around this very spot. Whoever it was, they'd broken the law, and intentionally sabotaged our security. Was it too much of a stretch for them to be the people responsible for cursing Madame Grey and the other victims, too? Maybe, maybe not, but the fact that we had no leadership right at the same time as intruders had entered the town was a suspicious coincidence at best. I debated switching my fairy disguise back on again—then I spotted someone very familiar approaching.

Blythe's mother, Mrs Dailey.

I should have known.

Mrs Dailey was responsible for bringing the hunters into Fairy Falls. And she had way more magic than I did. All I had was my fairy magic... unless I sneaked up on her from behind. But if she'd sensed I was here, I was in real trouble.

My hands shook as I reached for my wand. I'd memorised the sleeping spell Rita had used on Alissa, but I'd never tried it myself before. We hadn't got to that level of training yet. But if I drew Mrs Dailey's attention, she might turn me into a mouse or worse.

Moving as quietly as possible, I used a *hidden* spell to make myself unobtrusive. It'd fail the instant she actually spotted me, but it'd be easier to sneak up on her. She didn't openly carry her wand, which surprised me. I thought she of all people would be cautious when walking alone in the woods, considering she was older and more sensible than I was, but she was also wildly unpredictable. What was she scheming?

As she walked, I moved in behind her and cast the sleeping spell Rita had used on Alissa.

Mrs Dailey didn't react at all, and the trees barely stirred. *Did I remember it wrong?*

I tried again. My wand lit up, showing that it was definitely working. Had she blocked me? Or used a protective spell on herself? If she'd used a warding spell, I'd probably have to get up close to undo it. She'd spot me instantly.

Right. Get the police. Or Rita.

But if I turned my back, I'd lose sight of her, and I might never be able to prove she planned to meet with the hunters here. Of course, she'd probably claim innocence, but surely she wouldn't have gone to the trouble of casting a protection spell on herself if she didn't expect trouble.

I kept following behind her, casting spell after spell, but she gave no indication she'd felt a thing. Not so much as a rustle in the bushes. Must be a ward. It'd take real-life handcuffs to trap her, which I didn't have.

I reached into my pocket for my phone. To call the police, I'd have to walk away so she wouldn't overhear, unless I used magic on something else to trap her in place. I could snap a picture of her wandering suspiciously around the woods with my phone, but I'd left the sound turned on. So much for technology saving the day. Unless… the problem was my wand.

One way to find out. I aimed my wand at the tree in front of her, angling it so she'd think the spell came from the opposite direction, and fired off a spell. The air current knocked a branch loose, which disintegrated before it hit the ground in front of her.

Mrs Dailey spun around, and I held my breath, but she headed down the path opposite mine, her sharp gaze searching the bushes. I kept backing up, my feet feather-light on the ground. She scanned the clearing, and when I glimpsed her face, her expression looked positively murderous.

Several tense moments later, she turned her back on the clearing and strode haughtily down the forest path. I remained out of sight, breathing fast. She hadn't seen me. Part of me wished I'd had the nerve to get a picture of her with that terrifying look on her face, but she'd probably have broken my phone, or told the police I'd sneaked up on *her* instead of the other way around. If she knew I'd come to her house without permission, that'd be it for me.

I stopped for long enough to allow her to get a good distance down the path, then tailed her, not daring to move too close behind in case she spotted me. Her path wove through the trees down a route I knew, towards the entrance to the forest I'd followed the elf through.

Movement rustled the branches and a huge gargoyle came into view. He was huge, and stone-coloured, with massive leathery wings and an intimidating expression. My paranormal sixth sense showed me images of stone cliffs and sharp claws, and I swallowed hard. *Please let him be on the side of the law, not hers.*

I half expected Mrs Dailey to turn back to avoid him, but instead she kept going. If I followed any closer, I'd be spotted, and I had no idea what game she was playing now.

Mrs Dailey nodded a greeting to the gargoyle as she passed by. So the police knew she was here. Either she'd gained their trust, or she was covering her tracks.

Right, here we go.

"Hello?" I said loudly. "Is anyone out here?"

Mrs Dailey halted mid-step and turned around. The gargoyle's ears pricked up. "Who's out there?"

"Oh, there's someone here! I thought I was lost for good."

I walked out onto the path, schooling my face into puzzlement and relief. Both of them stared at me.

"I'm lost," I said. "I went for a walk and got lost. Can you tell me the way out?"

The gargoyle grunted and jerked his head over his shoulder. "Right there. Haven't you learned your lesson about wandering around the woods alone?"

"I thought there wasn't anything in the woods that shouldn't be," I said innocently. "The monster is dead, right? And it looks like the police have plenty of people on security duty."

Mrs Dailey narrowed her eyes at me. "What are you doing in here?"

"Gathering spell ingredients," I said, trying a smile. "What about you?"

"None of your business."

My acting wasn't great, but she couldn't prove I'd been following her. Nor did it sound like the police were in the know about her little scheme. But since I was the only person who'd seen her, my word wouldn't be enough to prove her guilt, especially as I hadn't actually seen her break the law. With Madame Grey gone, I didn't dare issue a direct challenge, and it was downright alarming that she'd already done something to remove the town's security so that her hunter friends could get in. Of course, with the gargoyle present, she couldn't say anything that might give away why she'd actually been in the forest herself.

"It's not illegal to walk in the woods, is it?" I asked, when she glared at me. "I was just making friendly conversation."

She grunted and walked away. I didn't follow, not wanting to push my luck.

"I thought you were leaving," said the gargoyle.

"I did come here to gather ingredients." I waited until Mrs Dailey was out of hearing, then I said, "I was actually here with Nathan, but he had to leave. Something about hunters breaching our security and wandering into the woods. He sent me to tell the police." He'd probably called the office himself by now, but it wouldn't hurt to let someone else know.

His brows shot up. "Hunters? A likely story."

He was one of Steve's lot. They never believed a word I

said no matter what proof I placed before them. "Ask Nathan when he comes back. He went to escort them to the border. You might want to check your patrols north of the woods."

He scowled. "Don't tell me how to do my job."

It was worth a try. "All right. I'll find my own way out."

I hoped he'd take my advice, and that Nathan would manage to get Sleepy, Dopey and Grumpy out of town without too much of a fuss. But Blythe's mother had invited them in, and whatever ward she'd used on herself was seriously strong. I couldn't trap her with witch magic, and as much use as my lie-sensing ability had been when catching criminals, it wouldn't be of any help if nobody believed me to begin with. She was too clever, and she'd covered her tracks. Who knew what she might be planning to do when Madame Grey didn't show up for tomorrow's council meeting? Worse, I had no ingredients, pixie dust included. And even if I had, the tracking spell would take two days to brew. Two days I didn't have. Mrs Dailey might be planning to strike before then.

I left the forest and texted Nathan asking him to speak to me when he got back from escorting the hunters out of town. There was no way to bring Mrs Dailey to the police's attention without making myself look equally suspicious, and I was woefully short on allies. I hoped Alissa had stayed put in the flat, at least.

I walked slowly, then picked up the pace. I was tired and hungry and irritated at the universe in general. How had I ended up facing a criminal alone again? I couldn't even go into the woods without accidentally running into people breaking the law. Then again, Nathan had also been a witness to the hunters' presence, but I didn't know how he planned to handle them, short of calling the police and hoping the three trespassers didn't sneak back in. And I could trust Steve to handle them with as much finesse as Sky the cat with a pile of bubble wrap.

Nathan responded to my message—*I'm on my way. Will talk to you in person.*

I couldn't tell his tone from the message, or whether he was annoyed with me for getting in the way. We still hadn't talked our issues through, and when we'd spoken, it'd been as though the last few weeks hadn't happened at all. Did he forgive me for deceiving him, or had he kept his distance because he thought I was mad at *him* for jailing my father? I should talk to him about it, but then I'd have to get into my quest for the elf king, and besides, there were a lot more important matters we needed to deal with first. Like the future of the town's safety, for instance. It was easier, if frustrating, to worry about Nathan, but even my love life was a paranormal mess.

I let myself into the flat. Alissa remained in her room, and Roald hung around dejectedly. With Sky still missing, I gave Roald his share of attention, and got up when the doorbell rang.

"No trouble?" I asked Nathan.

"I talked to the border guards," he said. "They were knocked out. I reported it to Steve, but you know how adept he is at handling things beyond his control. Judging by the state of the scene, it was a spell that knocked them out, but not one that could be traced to its caster."

"It's Blythe's mother," I said quietly. "She showed up right where the hunters were supposed to meet the person who hired them." I explained what I'd seen and how I'd decided to try to call her out in front of the police. Not that it'd worked in the end.

"That was a good idea, regardless," he said. "She can't accuse you of wrongdoing at least. I hope the gargoyle took your advice, but if not, there'll be more of them at the forest border shortly, from what they said to me on the phone."

"You didn't tell the werewolves, did you?"

"Definitely not," Nathan said. "I realise they deserve to know that outsiders trespassed on their territory, but they did so at the command of someone from Fairy Falls itself, someone trying to destabilise the peace. With no proof, it's best to keep the matter between ourselves and the police."

I turned this over in my mind. "Yeah, we *really* need proof. You guys don't do security cameras, do you?"

"There are naked shifters running around the woods all the time," he said. "The gargoyles would be traumatised if they had to view the footage."

The humour was a surprise, and I cracked up laughing. "Yeah, all right, I see it. I was going to snap a picture of Blythe's mother doing her Evil Witch stare, but I forgot to turn the sound off on my phone. I know glaring isn't a criminal offence. She just looked plain evil, though. Had her fangs out and everything, metaphorically speaking. Like a cross between Professor Umbridge and the Terminator."

He smiled a little at that, though there was still a tightness to his expression. "You're very lucky you weren't spotted, considering."

Considering what? I'm a fairy? Had he seen me de-glamoured? I'd moved quickly, but I was also shedding glitter everywhere again. No wonder Blythe's mother had looked so bewildered. And Nathan himself, for that matter. I looked like I'd come back from a party at the student halls.

"Yeah, I'm glad she didn't see me," I said. "But I have no idea how to bring her to justice with no proof. It's not a crime to go for a walk by the falls, and it's not like she and the hunters actually crossed paths."

"She's absolutely committed crimes," he said. "Usually there's some evidence, but we'd need a warrant to search her house, and if she's friendly with the police…"

"She's not friendly with anyone. We have that going for us." I looked over my shoulder at the house. "And I'm guessing she cursed everyone who got in her way, though I can't think how she got to Alissa. I don't want to confront her alone. She'd turn me into a mouse."

"Yes, I wouldn't do anything hasty. Even a public confrontation might go wrong."

"I don't want to sit back and do nothing either," I said. "Look… what about the hunters? You don't think they'll try to sneak back in?"

"I made my opinions clear to Steve, and he's sending more gargoyles to the border specifically to search them out."

"She might try the same trick again," I said. "I was worried they might try to jump you in the woods. I can't believe they walked right through shifter territory, though. That wasn't very bright of them. You knew one another before? All three of them?"

He grimaced. "Look—Blair, we should talk about this somewhere else."

"I'd invite you in, but Alissa's sleeping off her angry hangover. Angover."

He shook his head, his mouth twitching. "Blair, want to come with me to the Troll's Tavern?"

He was asking me out. I gave myself a mental shake. No, he wasn't, he wanted to talk somewhere the perpetrators wouldn't run into us, or where we might accidentally disturb the neighbours.

"I would, but I think they'll kick me out for spreading glitter everywhere."

"Isn't there a spell for that?" he asked.

"Right. Yeah, there is." Flustered, I went for my wand. To my intense surprise, I actually got the cleaning spell right on the first go and the glitter disappeared. Maybe I wasn't a total disaster of a witch after all.

———

It wasn't a date, but our sojourn to the Troll's Tavern was better than our last one. Both of us were distracted, but at least we weren't surrounded by fiercely efficient witch security guards this time. Nathan and I found a table tucked into a corner and ordered by tapping the menu, same as usual. When the food showed up, I dug in, suddenly ravenous. Chasing criminals really worked up an appetite.

"How do we get the police to see you-know-who is the guilty one?" I asked Nathan over drinks. "She'll deny everything I saw, and even then, I didn't see her actually do anything illegal. She just stood there in the forest and waited. I tried to drop a branch on her and it fell to pieces. What sort of ward is that?"

His brows shot up. "You tried to drop a branch on her?"

"In front of her," I amended. "I was trying to work out if she put the ward on the forest or on herself."

"On herself, I imagine," he said. "I have to admit, I didn't think a non-council witch was behind this."

"You knew it was her?" I asked. "Because… you traced the call, right? Isn't that proof enough?"

He shook his head. "The hunters told me they got a call from a Mrs Johnson asking them to apply to Dritch & Co. But the people who got that call weren't in the same department as the people I ran into today."

"Mrs who?" I said blankly. Oh, no. Someone else had called them?

"I'll find out," he said, taking a sip of his beer. "A witch, I'd guess."

"Maybe one of Blythe's mother's friends," I said. "She must have allies to have pulled off a scheme like this. That, or she used an alias. I can't believe she brought down the security, let alone convinced three people to trespass into the werewolves' forest. Do the rest of the hunters know they came here?"

"Not if they were acting on their own account," said Nathan. "There aren't strict rules on what members can or can't do when they're not working, and each para-normal community has different laws on whether or not hunters are allowed to enter their town or village."

"Those guys didn't seem like the cerebral sort either."

"The office people are a different bunch," he said. "I should know, I worked there."

I sipped my drink. "I thought you used to work in the prison. And as a security guard, unless that was the same?"

"I've worked in a few different departments," he said. "I never felt... settled, or that any particular position fit me right. In the end, I decided apprehending paranormal criminals wasn't for me."

"Then—how did you get into it in the first place? It's not exactly something you see on job application websites. Even in the paranormal world. You mentioned your family were involved, right?"

"They are," he confirmed. "My family actually runs that branch. My dad did, but he retired, leaving it to my brother. I didn't tell you the details before because I thought it would bore you, but there's a chance you might end up meeting them in person if they decide the town's situation is serious enough to send people in."

"Really? They'd do that?"

I'd sort of hoped that the 'meeting the parents' part of our relationship would involve fewer trespassing incidents and even fewer nefarious witches trying to bring down the covens. I was finally getting to know him, though, which counted for something.

"Let's hope it won't come to that," he said. "I hope that the police will take *my* report seriously, but the paranormal hunters can send people to wherever they like if they think there's a serious issue."

"With what?" I asked. "It's not like those thick-headed numbskulls could actually run a paranormal town... uh. No offence to your family."

"Oh, they're as thick as stumps," he said, surprising me. "My brothers, that is. There's a reason my mother left."

I didn't laugh. I was too surprised. His family was broken up, too?

"You said you had a little sister, right?"

He nodded. "Yes. She's a novice hunter. I don't think she'll stick with it, but she's still at the stage where she wants to impress her older brothers. My family has a history of being paranormal sensitives with a specific set of skills so it's inevitable that almost all of us ended up working for the hunters, because short of working for paranormals without being one of them, there aren't many other options. My mother was from a small paranormal village herself. She was a witch with little skill, and when she met my dad, she decided to move away."

"So that's why..." He'd related to me off the bat. And I'd screwed everything up by not trusting him, even when he'd given me no reason to believe that he'd judge me. I'd been a real fool.

"That's why what?" he asked.

I shook my head. "Nothing. I wish I'd asked you more about your family before. It just felt hypocritical when I know so little about mine."

"Right," he said, and I wondered if he was thinking the same.

"So what was it like growing up with them?" I asked.

"It's like growing up paranormal, but not exactly," he said, seeming to relax a little. "The paranormals themselves tolerate us on the whole, but there's a fair few who don't like us—for good reason. I was always aware of that, but I'd met quite a few people from Fairy Falls in my time as a hunter. I travelled into the forest before and befriended the pack."

"Wait, the same pack who... don't like hunters?"

He grimaced. "There was an incident with a rogue. Not from this town. The pack is friendly with several others in the area, and unfortunately, one of those packs had a member who broke the law and attacked a human. I was sent with the hunters to bring him in, and the friends of the werewolf in question never forgave me for it. But I'm still on speaking terms with several other shifters who don't see things that way. I just have to avoid the family who runs the pack when I'm here."

"So that's why you can walk onto their territory in the forest without getting eaten alive."

"There's also the law," he said dryly. "It does work, most of the time. I don't know how you have such a knack for running into the rare exception."

"I used to attract havoc constantly in the normal world, too," I admitted. "Not sure whether it's down to being half fairy and half witch, but I've moved on so many times that I'm still expecting to get kicked out of here, too."

"That won't happen," he said.

My insides fluttered. Yes… the feelings were definitely still there.

"Your wand's stopped acting up," he observed. "Didn't you say you used it to drop a branch on Mrs Dailey?"

I glanced down at my drink. "Yeah. It's like I thought—I'm left-wand-handed. Right for the fairy magic."

"Is that the reason for the glitter?" he asked. "You don't have to tell me."

You know what? I wanted to. "I was practising de-glamouring. Before I ran into you-know-who." My mood sobered. "She must have allies in town. If the hunters got a phone call from someone who wasn't her. But I thought she hated all the covens."

"Maybe she has others on her side who share her viewpoint," he said.

That's what I'd feared. Blythe's family might have cut ties with the council, but now they might have proof that the boundaries of the town weren't adequately guarded. And it was one step from that to bringing the hunters in and undoing the peace that had existed here for so long.

"Madame Grey is missing," I said quietly. "She fell under the same curse as Alissa did. I was going to make up a tracking spell to find her, but I don't have the ingredients, and it takes two *days* to brew."

Nathan put down his glass. "So that's why you were in the woods?"

"Sort of." The lie felt worse than I'd expected, considering it might easily have been the truth. "I sent my cat on a mission to gather ingredients for the spell, but he kept me waiting an hour. Probably went to visit his vampire friend. But she's gone. I don't know where she is. Don't… spread that around. Rita wants to keep it quiet."

"I suspected something might be wrong," he said. "Madame Grey is usually more responsive to contact. I tried to leave messages for her earlier, but she never called back. That explains why."

"Yeah, sorry. I should have told you," I said. "But— that's why I didn't report Mrs Dailey. Another reason. Madame Grey would believe me, but how are we supposed to be able to set up a trial with the leading witch missing?"

"We can't," Nathan said. "And with the hunters camping outside town, it's only a matter of time before someone notices. It's lucky they left, and I hope they have the sense to stay away."

I wouldn't count on it, considering how little sense

those three hunters had demonstrated by coming here to begin with.

"There's a council meeting tomorrow," I said. "I'm going—I think. Someone needs to tell the coven leaders what she did. But with Madame Grey missing, there aren't many people who'd take my word for it. I need to find her."

"I'd advise you not to use any kind of tracking spell tonight, even if you manage to make one," he said. "You're tired and frustrated, and for all you know, Madame Grey is still in town and won't thank you for disturbing her at night."

Remembering how grumpy the new Alissa was, I had to admit he had a point. But it felt like the longer I waited, the closer Blythe's mother got to... whatever she planned to do.

"All right, first thing tomorrow, then."

I'd take proof—the little I had—directly to the council, and we'd find Madame Grey before the town fell apart.

14

Nathan walked me to the end of the road before taking out his phone. "The police want to speak to me."

"Are you going to tell them it was Mrs Dailey?"

He hesitated. "It's probably best to tread carefully for now. But I'll tell them clearly that the hunters planned to meet someone from the town in the forest. They'll work out from that that it's likely to be a witch."

"Will they, though?" I said. "Come on, you know Steve couldn't put two and two together with a calculator."

He frowned at his phone screen. "Yes, but some of the others will pick up on the hint. I hope. Either way, I'm expecting trouble tomorrow."

"At the council meeting." Despite myself, I wanted to go after Madame Grey tonight. If she wasn't at home, maybe she was somewhere else within reach. It wasn't as though I couldn't fly around town and search for her. If Steve the Gargoyle wasn't such a sceptic, I'd be able to get the police involved, too.

What was the point in being the only person who could sense lies if the law enforcement didn't believe me?

Yet despite everything, Nathan was on my side. I had to believe that together, we could stop Blythe's mother before she brought down the covens. And get a proper date at the end of it, too. Hey, I could dream.

It wasn't until Nathan had disappeared from sight that I remembered I never did get to the falls to find the pixie dust. Oh, well. That could wait. For all I knew, the elves were in league with Mrs Dailey as well. Nothing would surprise me at this point.

I turned the corner into the darkening street, and Mrs Dailey stepped out onto the path in front of me.

"Er… hi?" I said. "I thought you were going home."

Mrs Dailey's icy expression made me want to run for cover. The problem was, she was blocking my path.

"Er, do you mind moving out of the way? I need to get home."

"I'm afraid I can't let you do that, Blair," she said. "You might have fooled the ex-hunter into doing your bidding, but you're too unpredictable to be allowed to wander around unchecked."

My mouth went dry, and I regretted that last witch cocktail. "Um, excuse me?"

"I could read your pathetic little mind from the instant you came near me, you foolish child."

"You can read my thoughts." Stupid of me to assume she didn't have some sort of mind-reading power herself. Of course she'd hexed or cursed her own daughter, maybe to stop her from getting in the way. And now *I* was in her way, and if she blocked my powers—well, come to think of it, my powers weren't much use if people didn't believe me anyway.

No, she planned to do worse than that.

"Don't kill me!" I stepped back, wondering if I could reach the end of the road before she caught me.

"Kill you? Certainly not. But I should wipe your mind. I did the same to my ex-husband, too, you know. It's a final decision, but in your case, it's the right one to make. I wonder… would you like to live out the rest of your days believing you're a normal?"

No.

I snapped my fingers, switching on my fairy disguise and taking flight. Before I'd risen more than a metre, she splayed a hand and I found myself frozen. *No. Move, Blair!*

I didn't know enough fairy magic to escape.

"MIAOW."

Sky leapt in front of her, hissing angrily. While he was in his smaller form, he'd broken her concentration, and the spell let me go, causing me to fall back to earth. With a yowl, Sky attached herself to her leg, tearing and clawing. She swore and kicked out, and I took the opportunity to yell at the top of my lungs. Mrs Dailey stumbled back, still kicking out. *Ha. She forgot we're in public.* Sure enough, voices drifted down the road as people were drawn by the noise. She cast one furious glare at me and ran.

I breathed out, then all but flew in the direction of home. My whole body was trembling. Wiping memories *and* mind-reading was a lethal combination. But I had no proof she'd threatened me, and if I didn't bring any to the meeting tomorrow, the covens would never take my word over hers.

I let myself into the flat and sank onto the sofa, tears

stinging my eyes. Alissa was still in her room, and I was in even more trouble than before.

"Sky," I said distractedly. "Oh, Sky, this is all my fault."

"Miaow!" he admonished.

"It is. I'm going to end up on a train to NormalsVille with my memory wiped and she'll take over the town with the hunters and her allies."

He swatted at my arm, drawing blood. "Miaow."

"Oh, it's okay for you. You can just find someone else to adopt if I'm the one who gets kicked out of town."

"Miaow," he admonished.

"Yes, I know I'm being stupid. She could have killed me. Or wiped my memory. What's the use of being a fairy and a witch if I can't stop her?"

She wouldn't just have wiped my memories of tonight, but my memories of being a paranormal at all. I'd never find out what had really happened to my family, and I'd lose... everything.

I stroked Sky, desperately wishing I could speak to Alissa, but she wasn't even acting like herself at the moment. And Nathan... I had to stop running to him every time I needed reassurance. He was busy with the police—and my last hope to convince them of Mrs Dailey's treachery. No, I needed to deal with the council myself. If nothing else, Vincent was a mind-reader and would see my honesty. That had to count for something. Donovan, chief of the werewolf pack, hated me, but he hated the hunters even more. He'd never vote in their favour. Even Blythe might testify against her mother if I gathered enough support. She was the first victim, after all. Maybe I should call her and ask her to show up to the meeting, but her mother might be listening in.

So here I was, depending on vampires, the man I'd deceived, and my former nemesis. How had my life come to this?

———

After a restless night, I woke later than I'd planned, but with plenty of time to go Madame Grey-hunting before the council meeting. If the sun and the lack of a grumpy Alissa didn't put me in a better mood, the sight of the ingredients gathered on the table did. Sky had come through for me after all.

"Thanks," I said, rubbing him behind the ears as I prepared to set up the tracking spell. It'd take two days to brew, but in the meantime, my last shot at finding Madame Grey was to transport myself to her house and hope that she was actually there. Alissa was still dead to the world, and even if she tried to piggy-back on my spell, the bindings she was under stopped her from using transportation spells to get out of the flat. I'd used the spell a couple of times before, by imitating Madame Grey herself, but it wasn't one I'd practised a lot.

I waved my wand, carefully, and thought, *take me to Madame Grey's house.*

A flash enfolded around me, and I crashed headfirst into a high gate outside a large house. Ow. Madame Grey's house must be strongly warded, but at least I'd reached the right place. Rubbing my forehead, I took a few steps back from the gate, trying to see through to the windows, but the thick hedges blocked the way. Not my smartest move. It was probably too much to ask the council to postpone the meeting for the two days it would take to brew up the tracking spell, and even then, I'd probably find Madame Grey in a spell-addled state. I definitely needed to think before I acted.

"What are you doing here, Blair?"

I spun around. Rita approached, her red hair dishevelled and bangles jangling everywhere.

"Probably the same as you," I said. "Tried a transportation spell. Didn't work. Have you found her?"

"No," she answered. "And the others moved the meeting earlier in light of yesterday's events. It's in half an hour."

"They *what?* Do they know—wait, what happened yesterday?" I'd texted Nathan but told him not to tell the police that Mrs Dailey had tried to attack me until we had proof of her treachery.

"The town's security was breached," she said. "The shifters kicked up a fuss, and now they're saying one of their own is under a spell, too."

Callie. Oh, poor Callie. After all this, I wouldn't be surprised if her overprotective father stopped her from working at Dritch & Co at all.

"Nathan told me there'd been a breach, but not that it was that serious," I said half-truthfully. "But—Madame Grey. I can't get in to see her at home."

Her mouth pinched. "I know. I've been trying to track her all night. Sorry, Blair, I have to go to the meeting without her."

I walked alongside her, my mind whirling. I was *not* what you called a qualified witch, fairy or not, but I *had* to get into that meeting.

"Blythe's mother did it," I said. "She all but confessed

to me, but she's powerful, and—threatened to wipe my memories. I didn't even know that was possible."

"She confessed to you?" Rita's eyes widened in shock. "Why?"

"I ran into her walking in the woods," I said. "Long story. Anyway, I'm convinced she's behind the security breaches as well as the curse, not that I have proof of either. Whether she's behind either of those things or not, it was enough for her to threaten to wipe my memory and turn me into a normal. I think she's plotting against the council and trying to convince them to bring the hunters in."

"Do you have proof? Without it, you'll be the one jailed, and telling the council won't solve anything." Her manner was distracted. "I'm sorry. I believe you, Blair, but Madame Grey was the strongest voice on the council and the others don't know who you are. The others might not *like* Mrs Dailey, but with no proof..."

They wouldn't believe me. Then the next chance she got, Mrs Dailey would corner me and finish the job.

"The meeting," I said, dropping my voice as we passed a group of witches. I hardly noticed if they stared or not. "Is there absolutely no chance they'll let me in? At all?"

I needed to at least see who might be working with the enemy if I wanted to get Mrs Dailey behind bars where she belonged. But if it ended badly, Blythe's mother might get her way after all.

"No. I'm sorry, Blair. I'll do my best to make my concerns clear without endangering your life."

"She wants to dismantle the covens,' I whispered.

"She'll have to try a lot harder. Madame Grey isn't the only strong voice on the council."

We reached the witches' headquarters, and Rita opened the front door. My heart jolted as the growing crowd inside the lobby looked at me, as though I wore my fairy side on full display. A freak of nature.

The council was made of representatives from every paranormal group, not just witches.

I was done hiding behind a disguise.

I snapped my fingers, letting my wings unfold, and walked into the room which served as the meeting place, ignoring both the stares and Rita's admonishing look telling me to get out. Blythe's mother was nowhere to be seen. Neither was the leader of the werewolves, worryingly. I didn't like Chief Donovan and the feeling was mutual, but he'd never support bringing the hunters here. Was he still dealing with Callie?

"Where is Madame Grey?" demanded one of the witches. "We cannot start this meeting without her."

"She's not here," I said, taking a seat at the large table that dominated the room. "You're all going to drive her into an early grave with all your complaining. She's been doing nothing but running meetings for weeks since the incident with the vampires and werewolves."

Once again, I was eternally grateful that I had the ability to tell little white lies after all.

The witches muttered to one another across the table. Then protests broke out. "This meeting is for coven leaders only. What are you even doing here? You're not a qualified witch."

"Not a witch at all," said one very loud whisper.

"Yeah, you're right," I said. "I'm a fairy. Since I'm the only fairy in the town, I can represent myself on the council, right? You have representatives from all the other paranormal groups, but not fairies."

More muttering followed. Rita's expression was torn between annoyance and exasperation, but underneath, I swore she looked impressed. I was right, though. I mean, most of them didn't look like they believed I was serious, but they couldn't argue with my logic.

"She's right," said Rita. "She can represent the fairies. It's in the rulebook."

The witches scowled and whispered, but their angry glares didn't bother me nearly as much as the idea of Blythe's mother getting what she wanted without me being here to stop her. The woman herself was conspicuously absent, more so than Madame Grey, but of course nobody in this room knew what she was plotting. She must have allies here, but I didn't know the coven leaders well enough to be sure who else might be scheming.

"As for the meeting," Rita said, "Madame Grey needs to be present for the final vote, but today's discussion concerns our future security measures, given the state of things."

The others began to chime in. They'd heard about the security breach, but apparently the police hadn't told anyone that the guards had been knocked out. They made it sound like nobody had bothered to check the boundaries at all. Worryingly, more people supported the idea of bringing in non-paranormals than I'd thought.

"It's vital that we protect the town by any means necessary," said a witch who bore a striking resemblance to Nina. Wait—her mother, who'd started her own coven.

"Even if it means destroying the peace?" asked Vincent. "We all know that the hunters are more inclined towards hunting down definite criminals, not policing the streets of a town which has a low crime rate under normal circumstances. There's likely to be misunderstandings, and with the hunters, that might prove fatal."

I knew I could count on the leading vampire to represent the interests of the people more likely to fall victim to misunderstandings with the hunters, even if he didn't care much for the werewolves.

The door flew open, and everyone turned to stare as Blythe's mother strode in.

"The only criminal in this room is Blair Wilkes," she said.

15

Everyone gaped at her. Their expressions ranged from shock to hostility.

"You can't be in here," said Rita. "You rejected the covens and resigned from the council."

Murmurs of agreement rose. *Oh, good. They don't like her.*

"I'm here to reclaim my position," Mrs Dailey responded. "In Madame Grey's absence, there's a need for an impartial perspective, and an even bigger need for someone to take control of the situation before someone else brings their criminal ways into the town."

"Uh, Peter the wizard was *from* Fairy Falls," I pointed out. "I can't say I know where he got the monster from, but unless you're suggesting setting the hunters on innocent people as a precaution, you're not going to find many people who'll agree with your approach."

Her eyes narrowed as she walked down the table to an empty seat, but she kept up her professional act in front of the gathering witches. "How many of you have felt unsafe on your own streets? Blair herself was the killer's target and narrowly escaped death in front of her own house."

How did she even know about that? Had she been talking to Steve? I'd faced more danger from *her* down the road from my own house. Besides, bringing in people like those idiot hunters wouldn't have stopped Peter's rampage. He'd been too powerful.

"Peter was a wizard," I said, since nobody else responded to her words. "He could have turned all the hunters into frogs in a second. Trust me, bringing humans —*normals*—in isn't going to solve our problems."

"That wasn't my suggestion," she said. "I rather think the coven system should be replaced with a new one. It's impossible to represent everyone, especially some of our more… unusual citizens." Her gaze lingered on me, and heat crept up my neck. "An outside committee might be exactly what we need. The hunters' standards are iron-clad, and much more extensive than Madame Grey's lax approach."

Quiet mutters broke out. Some of the witches sounded like they were considering her words, and the truth in them. My heart dropped. She really did want to bring down the covens—and some of the other witches might have been waiting for this very opportunity.

Now wasn't the time for caution. Madame Grey wouldn't want anyone to outright forget her, and besides, if we didn't expose Mrs Dailey's curse, anyone else might be next.

"Er, Madame Grey is *missing*," I said, interrupting the murmur of voices. "She's not skiving off, nobody has seen her in days. If anything's happened to her, shouldn't the police be looking for her?" I should have thrown caution aside and called them myself, but Steve probably wouldn't have believed me. Or he'd have found a way to make it my fault.

"Missing?" repeated an elderly witch.

"Someone cursed her," I said. "They cursed her grand-daughter, too."

"If she has fallen victim to an accident, then shouldn't it be her family's responsibility to take care of her and inform the council of the situation?" asked Mrs Dailey.

"Not if she's been cursed by another witch and driven out of town," I said. "My flatmate Alissa is under the same curse, if you want proof. And my boss."

"Curses?" repeated Mrs Dailey, turning to me. "And who exactly do you accuse of cursing people in such a manner?"

She was all but goading me into making an open accusation, knowing I wouldn't be able to convince anyone with no evidence to speak of. I hadn't wanted to make the accusation public for precisely that reason. Rita was right —she could easily make my life a living hell if I did so, assuming she didn't just wipe my memory and be done with it. But the alternative was keeping quiet and letting her twist the minds of everyone else in the room until they ousted their own leader without even looking for her.

"I don't know yet," I said—technically true. "But the timing strikes me as odd. And so does the decision to put anything to a vote with your leader missing. Shouldn't you at least wait until she comes back before taking drastic action?"

"Nobody said anything about drastic action," said Mrs Dailey.

Damn her. For all her dramatic entrances, she hadn't actually done anything yet. I had nothing to go by except Alissa, and I'd bound her to the flat. And nobody in this room really knew her well enough to be certain she'd been cursed.

"I'm just pointing out that several people from this town are under a curse," I said. "For instance, my boss. Veronica Eldritch."

"Can she speak for herself?" asked Mrs Dailey, now paying full attention to me. Or pretending to, anyway. She knew she had me.

"No, because she's missing. She abandoned her business overnight and took off. And so did Callie, Chief Donovan's daughter."

"He's absent today," said Blythe's mother. "Convenient."

"He's absent because he's probably looking for her," I said, exasperated. "My flatmate Alissa will speak to you— Rita knows she's cursed."

All eyes turned to Rita, who dipped her head. "As of yet, we haven't been able to determine the cause, but Alissa seems to be under a personality altering curse."

"Personality altering?" said Mrs Dailey. "That doesn't strike me as potentially dangerous."

It does if it causes the person in charge to run out of town.

"I suppose it shouldn't surprise me that Miss Wilkes would make those accusations," she said. "She's the daughter of a criminal, after all."

My body stiffened. "Excuse me, what?"

How did she know about my father? I'd thought nobody did, least of all Blythe's family.

"You don't know?" she said, with the hint of a laugh in

her voice. "I suppose I can't blame you for your ignorance, but your parents were common thieves. With that in mind, forgive me if I find your accusations hard to believe."

My mouth hung open. She'd come out one step ahead of me after all. And—as far as my lie-sensing power indicated, she was telling the truth.

"I don't see what Blair's parentage has to do with anything," said Rita delicately. She looked outraged on my behalf, but if Mrs Dailey had wanted to divert the others' attention from any accusations I might direct towards her, she'd succeeded. Most of them hadn't wanted me in the meeting anyway.

"Blair seems to have got it into her head that I cursed her friend," said Mrs Dailey. "Nonsense, I'm sure you'll agree. She had a ridiculous disagreement with my daughter at her workplace and it escalated. A childish argument that resulted in my daughter's wand being bound by this very council."

Whispers sounded among the witches. They did remember her. Everyone knew Blythe had had her wand bound—after all, it was the council who'd passed the final sentence against her. They should also know *why* she'd been bound—for hexing her own colleague—but more important had been the fact that she'd accidentally sabotaged an investigation in order to get me fired.

Despite that, there were too many people nodding at Mrs Dailey's words.

"She's telling the truth," Vincent said. "I for one vote against the added security, however, though my mind might change if Madame Grey doesn't show up by the vote on Friday. As for the accusations, I have no opinion.

Blair seems to believe her friend was cursed, but since that curse has no obvious effects, I imagine you'd have difficulty proving it was the case."

Vincent! The vampire had come out on *her* side. Had she paid him off? Surely not. He was a super-rich seven-hundred-year-old vampire. What could she possibly offer him? More likely, he was playing his own game and had decided not to tell any of us what it was. Great.

Unless I'd had it wrong, and Mrs Dailey wasn't responsible at all.

"Hang on," I said. "Has anyone seen Blythe Dailey? She got hit by the curse too. I'm pretty sure anyone who knows her will know she's acting out of character. She also lost her ability to read minds."

Mrs Dailey's nostrils flared. "Any issues affecting my family are our business only." She turned to Vincent. "You're quite right that no vote can take place without the presence of Madame Grey. If she's not present at tomorrow's meeting, I propose that we come to a decision about how to rearrange our leadership, and whether or not to bring in outsiders to help. Agreed?"

More muttering came from the witches. One thing was clear—they thought Madame Grey had left of her own accord. Mrs Dailey had exposed my story and seemed to prove it not to be true. And I had no leverage against her.

As the meeting broke up and the others began to filter out of the room, I made my way to Vincent.

"Why'd you do that?" I asked. "Do you want the hunters to stake all your people?"

"That woman," he said, "is in the right, according to

the law. You have no proof. But that doesn't mean she will win this."

"You let her win," I said. "I get that there's no proof. But now she's got her way, she's going to make even more absurd demands. The covens will collapse."

"She has two children—one under eighteen—under her roof. From what I picked up from her thoughts, she plans to use them as leverage if she doesn't get her way."

"What do you mean by that?" She wouldn't use them as a shield, right? Or who knew, maybe she would. She wanted to bring me down at any cost. "You know the only way to prove she did it is to kidnap Blythe from her own house, right? Which her mother has probably locked her in, I might add. That, or bring Alissa in, but she thinks there's nothing wrong with her and she'll hop on a broomstick and fly off the instant I take off the wards on the flat. The only person who saw what she did to me is my *cat*."

"Well, then," said Vincent. "That should be enough, no?"

And he was gone.

Think, Blair. Sky could technically get into Blythe's house, for all the good it'd do. But even if Blythe spoke against her mother, she had the council eating out of her hand now.

"Sky, I need you," I muttered.

Between one blink and the next, the little cat was there, sitting at my feet.

"Sky, can you unlock Blythe's house?"

"Miaow."

"Right." If Mrs Dailey used a transportation spell of her own, she'd catch up to us, fast. The others were leaving the hall. This was the only chance I'd get. I walked quickly out of the hall, heading for an empty classroom.

"Blair!" Nina ran up to me, her eyes frantic. "Can I speak to you for a moment?"

"Er, now's not a good time."

"Please. It's about—Mrs Dailey. She…"

"Your mother supported her."

"She forced her." Her voice dropped to a whisper. "She wiped my mum's memory and threatened to do the same to me."

My heart sank. "I believe you. I'm going to get evidence that she cursed Madame Grey, right now. Can you stall her before she leaves? Say anything, get her to stay in plain sight, but don't endanger your life."

She nodded. "Yeah, I can."

"Thank you." I ran into the deserted classroom and cast the transportation spell.

In a flash, I landed in front of Blythe's gate. This time, it was closed, and a green shimmer told me it was warded. Like the wizard's house had been. Blood wards? If I was related to her family, maybe they'd let me in.

I put my hand on the gate and felt a sharp pain sting my palm. Ow. Twisting around, I saw no sign of Sky.

Oh, no. Had the spell only worked on me and not him?

"Blair!" called Rebecca, leaning out of the downstairs window of the house. "What are you doing here?"

"Looking for Blythe."

"She's gone," she said dismally. "You have to leave, or mum will catch you. It's all my fault."

My throat went dry. "What did she do?"

Rebecca took in a breath. "It was me who cursed

everyone. And now my mother's going to ruin everything because of me."

I stared at her for a moment. "I'm sorry, what? You did it?"

"I didn't mean to." She squeezed her eyes shut. "Blythe was annoying me again, and I... you know, I've always been able to influence people's moods, but it took me forever to figure it out. It's why my mum didn't know I had any magical talent. But it went out of control. I used it on Blythe to change her mood because she was always yelling at me. It's like... I can't describe it, but it's as though I got into her mind, suggesting that she'd be happier if she was less unfriendly. I didn't expect it to shut out her mind powers, too, but she always hated hearing everyone's thoughts all the time and I thought she preferred it that way."

My mouth fell open. "Really?"

She dropped her gaze. "Yeah. I kept it quiet, but she found out—my mum found out, and said she was going to use my powers to take down the council. I didn't know anyone who might help, so I went to Blythe's work place—"

"You did? But... I thought Blythe did."

She flushed. "Er, I disguised myself as Blythe. A basic charm. Not a good one, but it's like my ability just sort of hits everyone I come into contact with. I didn't know I'd done anything until that receptionist got angry, and the other woman ran off. I tried chasing after her, but I wasn't fast enough, and I didn't know how to undo it anyway. Then my mum caught me and dragged me home. Blythe didn't know I'd gone there, nor that I'd cursed them. I didn't tell her."

My head spun. She was being honest. I hadn't known. And—that meant Mrs Dailey had told the truth. She hadn't cursed anyone, just taken advantage of the situation.

"And—Alissa?" I asked.

"She was there when I went looking for you. Again— my mum caught me. And now she's made it so I *can't* leave the house."

I took a step toward the gate. "We're going to have to go to the council. Before she comes back."

"Before who comes back?" said Mrs Dailey from behind me.

16

"Get away from my house, Blair," said Mrs Dailey. "This is your last warning."

"You're holding your child hostage," I said. "Come on, did you really expect this to work out well for you? The covens won't disband because you said so."

"I can use my power on anyone," she said. "I cannot be touched by any hostile spell, either. And my dear daughter is unable to affect me with her own ability, which is the only reason that I took so long to notice what she could do. To think she chased off the covens' leader without any prompting. Imagine what she could do if she accessed her gifts to their full capacity."

Rebecca's hands pressed to her mouth and she let out a whimper. I tried to give her a look that conveyed calm or reassurance, but my heart hammered at a mile a minute. Where was Sky? If she wiped my memory, I'd lose everything, and so would her daughter. Not to mention the rest of the town.

Rebecca lowered her hands and yelled, "She's using an

amulet! If you get it off her, you'll be able to use a spell on her."

Mrs Dailey made a noise of irritation, pointed her wand at the window, and it snapped shut. Rebecca fell back with an inaudible shriek, while I took a step backwards, thinking hard. Rebecca had no wand. It was all up to me.

"If you touch me, I'll wipe your memory, Blair. I already took care of that cat of yours."

Oh no, Sky. She must have spelled him before she came here. She'd seen right through me all along.

I went for my wand, and she fired a spell in my direction. I jumped into the air, wings beating—*how* had I forgotten I had them out? Some fairy I was.

Mrs Dailey fired another spell, and I flew to the side in a flutter of wings and glitter. With my left hand, I pulled out my wand and waved it wildly in the best imitation of the time I'd accidentally conjured a disco ball into the flat. A burst of light ignited, and glitter streamed from my wand into the sky.

Nobody would be able to miss it. If there really were more gargoyles flying on patrol than usual, there was no way they wouldn't spot the explosion of light.

Mrs Dailey yelled in rage as glitter rained down on her. Being covered in pink and purple sprinkles made her look a lot less scary. "What are you doing, you incompetent mess of a witch?"

"Drawing attention," I said. "Nice try, but you can't run away from the law."

"Get down here, fairy!"

I flew higher, dodging her spells. Narrowing her eyes, she waved her wand, and vanished. Ah. A transportation spell. Luckily, she'd left a trail of glitter behind her.

Dark shapes appeared in the sky—gargoyles. They hadn't missed the light display.

"Hey, get over here!" I yelled. "Blythe's mother tried to attack me!"

"She did! I saw her." Blythe herself ran uphill, a panicked expression on her face. So she hadn't run off after all.

Three gargoyles descended to land in front of the house. "What is going on here?"

"Did you see that woman vanish?" I asked, pointing at the glittery mess she'd left behind. "She was attacking me."

"We saw," said the second gargoyle. "Mrs…"

"Dailey," I finished. "You saw her, right?"

They looked around. "Where did she go?"

"Very good question," I muttered. "She wouldn't have gone far. She locked up her house and trapped her daughter in there."

"She did," confirmed Blythe, looking very pale. "Please —find her."

Two of the gargoyles took flight while the third moved in on the house. "I can't get through this ward."

"I can," said Blythe. "It's only a blood ward, but she put worse on the house itself."

"Explain," the gargoyle growled.

I did, or I tried to. Halfway through my rambled explanation, the two gargoyles returned. They held Mrs Dailey between them, who looked furious.

"Those blasted elves!" she yelled.

The elves? "Did they chase you out of the forest?" I

laughed, unable to help it, then froze at the murderous expression on her face. "You can't attack me."

"Can't I?"

A pressure burst behind my eyes, like when I sensed someone's paranormal type, but a hundred times more painful.

No. Get out.

A *snap* sounded, Mrs Dailey stumbled back like I'd shoved her, and the gargoyles moved in, restraining her.

I blocked her.

"What is going on here?" Steve ambled over, looking at the glitter-strewn ground and Mrs Dailey's struggling form.

"We're arresting this woman for attacking someone," said one of the gargoyles.

"And trapping her children in her house and plotting to overthrow the council," I added, my voice shaking. *I blocked her.*

Steve whirled on me. "Do you have proof?"

The gargoyle who'd spoken cleared his throat. "Well, we saw her attempting to shoot this… fairy out of the air."

"I have a name," I said.

"She threw glitter at me!" Mrs Dailey protested, now apparently playing the innocent act.

"In self-defence," I said. "She tried to wipe my memory. Look, get a witch over here and they'll tell you that she locked her children in that house on purpose."

"To protect them from the likes of you."

"That's not true!" Rebecca yowled from the window. "Try to undo that ward and you'll see."

Mrs Dailey's remaining control over the situation swiftly unravelled. One of the gargoyles produced a pair of handcuffs, while the other held her arms behind her back.

"She's also in possession of an illegal amulet," added Blythe, who was being surprisingly helpful for once. "But only she can undo the spell on the house."

"The witches are here!" shouted a gargoyle. Sure enough, the rest of the council climbed the hill, Rita among them.

With a muttered curse, Mrs Dailey turned her wand on the house. There was a flash, and the shimmering above the gate disappeared. One of the gargoyles swiftly relieved her of her wand, while another snapped the handcuffs on her. Rebecca emerged from the house as the witches caught up, while Blythe hovered beside the gate as though unsure what to do with herself.

"I put the curse on them!" Rebecca said. "I'm sorry."

As the gargoyles hauled her mother away, the witches stepped in and converged on Rebecca, leaving Blythe forgotten.

"What do you mean, you cursed everyone?" one of them asked.

Eventually, the explanation came out. It was obvious that Rebecca hadn't intended to cause any harm, and besides, she was only eleven years old.

"She needs a mentor," said Rita, who'd taken charge of the situation. "We can work that out when we find Madame Grey... how many other people were affected?"

"Blythe was the first," said Rebecca. "I tried to use my ability on my mother, but it didn't work. No idea why."

"Her personality's probably too set in its ways," said Rita.

"I think it's because of her own gift," I said. "She's seriously strong. Are you sure the gargoyles can handle her?"

It'd seemed that she'd given in too easily, but then again, her entire plan had hinged on her daughter keeping quiet. Now, there was no point in her trying to regain ground. She'd lost.

"I'm sure they can," Rita answered. "As for Madame Grey…

"I don't know where she is," admitted Rebecca. "I wish I did."

"Not with the High Fliers?" I suggested.

"I can help with that," said Vincent, appearing at our side—with Sky in his arms.

"Sky!" I said. "He's okay."

"He is. It's lucky fairy cats are resilient."

"Miaow." Sky jumped out of his arms and ran to rub himself around my legs. I scratched behind his ears, relieved beyond measure.

I looked up at the vampire. "Did you say you know where Madame Grey is?"

"Sleeping in one of my coffins," said Vincent. "I assumed she wanted to get away from all the noise."

"Sleeping… you *knew?*"

Which meant Sky had known, too. *That cat.*

"I believe the girl will need to come with us to undo the spell," said Vincent.

"I'll come with her," said Rita, with a glance at the other witches. "Go back to the headquarters. I'll bring our leader back once the curse is undone."

Rita, Rebecca, Vincent and I made an odd group, especially with Blythe trailing along at the back since nobody had told her to leave. When we reached the vampires' headquarters beside the cemetery, it was to find Madame Grey emerging from the doors with a vacant expression on her face. "What is that racket? I was sleeping."

I grinned. If I were her, I'd have wanted to get away from the endless meetings, too. I imagined it'd been a nice break for her. And Alissa had got to relive her old dream once again. It wasn't all bad.

Blythe, on the other hand? Once the spell came off, she'd be back to her normal grumpy self.

Rebecca hesitantly approached the leading witch. "I'm sorry," she said. "I don't know how to undo it."

"Tell them to keep the noise down," responded Madame Grey. "I'm trying to sleep."

"We need you," I said. "Rita—how do you usually turn off a spell like that? I mean, it's not actually a curse either. Only Rebecca can do it."

But I knew so little about witches' latent talents, much less someone who'd likely been repressing it for years out of fear that her own mother would use it for nefarious reasons.

Rita shook her head. "It's like a switch in your head, I'm told."

"Yeah, that sounds right," I said. "Rebecca… maybe snap your fingers? That's how my fairy power works, but —you have to want to undo it."

Rebecca bit her lip. "I don't know how."

"Relax," Rita said. "Nobody is going to force you to use your magic against your will. Honest."

Rebecca seemed to pull herself together. Closing her eyes, she held out a hand. Then her eyes flew open and she gasped. "I've got it!"

Madame Grey turned slowly around to stare into the

vampires' headquarters, then wheeled back to face us. "What *am* I doing here?"

———

A very confusing hour later, we gathered in the meeting room again. Blythe's mother had been carted off to jail, which was no more than she deserved. There was undeniable proof that she'd broken at least half a dozen laws today alone. But her words remained in the back of my head—she thought my parents were thieves. Both of them, even. And she hadn't lied.

I'd removed the glitter, but kept my fairy wings out. At this point, I was past caring what anyone thought of me, and I was far from the centre of attention. Rebecca stood uncomfortably while Madame Grey asked her to demonstrate her powers again—this time, by removing the spell from a very reluctant Alissa. Luckily, Nina and her mother had volunteered to bring her in, because I had my hands full trying to get Blythe to stop trying to help out. Alissa snarled at everyone and tried to run, but Nina restrained her. The apologetic expression on her face suggested she was trying to make up for her mother's supporting Mrs Dailey, but I didn't blame either of them a bit.

"What the—" Alissa went still as Rebecca moved in closer. Then she stumbled backwards, looking utterly perplexed. "What am I doing here? Was I—flying?"

"You were cursed," I told her. "Not your fault."

"Oh, god, Blair. I'm sorry. I was awful to you."

"It was my fault," Rebecca said, hanging her head. "I

didn't mean to curse you. What's going to happen to me now?"

"You'll be fine," I told her. "Er… what about Blythe?" She was still there, hovering by the door with a weird smile on her face. "If anything, it's an improvement."

"I don't think she agrees." Rebecca walked to her sister. "Don't hate me for this, Blythe."

There was a brief pause. Blythe blinked, then utter horror crossed her face. I couldn't resist giving her a friendly wave, stifling laughter.

Blythe stumbled backwards and fled the room. Rebecca followed, with Rita on her tail, and I grinned to myself. If only magic could have frozen time for that instant, it'd have been perfect.

Madame Grey caught my arm, her expression back to its usual sharpness. "You did a great job today, Blair."

My grin faded. "Really, I kind of muddled through. What's going to happen with Rebecca's training?"

"She'll be given a mentor, naturally," said Madame Grey. "And we'll see to it that precautions are put into place that will ensure she won't use her power by accident again."

"I don't think her mother terrorising her helped much," I said quietly. "Uh—what about the council meeting? They were seconds from bringing in a new system. Not to mention the hunters."

She paused as though deliberating her words before saying, "I will make my position clear when we meet again for the vote tomorrow. Then we'll see."

Good. "Also, Veronica's missing," I added. "Is she in a coffin, too? And Lena, our co-worker, might have got hit as well."

"Good question," said Madame Grey, wearing an expression that dared everyone to laugh at the idea of the leading witch asleep in a coffin. On anyone else, it'd have looked sheepish, but she remained as dignified as ever, as though napping in coffins was perfectly normal. "I'll make a few calls and see."

While nobody dared laugh at her, I had an inkling that my transformation into a fairy was going to be replaced as the latest gossip in no time at all.

Dismissed, I left the hall. Blythe and her sister had gone, but Alissa waited for me outside the door.

"Sorry, Blair," she said. "I must have been a nightmare to deal with."

"Still better than Blythe on a good day," I said, which earned a chuckle. "Madame Grey is going to track down Veronica and Lena. I don't need that tracking spell after all."

"Oh, is that what you had those books out for?" asked Alissa.

"Yeah... the fairy one? Did you buy that? I'd have asked, but... well."

She shook her head. "No. I've never seen it before."

"Miaow."

I looked down at Sky. I suspected he'd sneaked off for a nap in the middle of the meeting, since this was the first I'd seen of him since Vincent had brought him to Blythe's house.

"You did it?" I asked the cat. "You stole the fairy book from the shop?"

"Miaow." He looked affronted.

"Right, you're friends with the bookshop staff." That, or he'd paid for it using my money. I wouldn't be surprised if he had. "You might have told me it was on the shelf. I needed that."

To find the pixie dust. Maybe now I'd finally get a moment's peace to fulfil the elf king's quest. I owed him double if it had been him who'd had his people chase Blythe's mother out of the forest, too.

Alissa nudged me. Nathan had entered the lobby. I hesitated, and she gave me another sharp jab with her elbow.

"Ow," I muttered. "I'm on it." No running away this time.

"Good," she said, and left me alone in the lobby.

Nathan spotted me. "Hey," he said. "I take it I missed all the action again?"

"Yeah, where were you?"

"I was with the police dealing with our hunter problem," he said. "Those three shouldn't be back anytime soon."

"Good," I said. "I take it someone filled you in on the latest drama?"

"Mostly," he said. "I saw them cart Mrs Dailey into the jail. Is Alissa back to normal?"

"Same as ever. So's Blythe." I looked down at Sky, but he'd vanished again. "I'm going to the falls now. Want to come with me? I'll tell you everything on the way."

"The falls? Sure. Any reason?"

"It's to do with my family." The words brought back what Blythe's mother had said. Yet another layer to the mystery… but once I found the pixie dust, I'd be one step closer to solving it.

I explained the events of that morning while Nathan and I walked through the town, and ended by admitting that Mrs Dailey had told the council both my parents were criminals.

"Obviously I don't know if she told the truth, but my lie-sensing ability told me she did," I finished, as we reached the path to the lake. "Was she right?"

"I'm sorry, I don't know," he said. "She might have deliberately been trying to get a rise out of you and warped the truth for her own ends."

"When have I been that lucky?" I turned away, towards the gilded surface of the lake. "I was just wrapping my head around the fact that my dad's in jail for who knows what crime, and now I find out *both* my parents might have been criminals. Why does everyone seem to know these things but me?"

"I wouldn't trust anything that woman says," he said. "What did you say you needed from the falls?"

"I didn't," I said. "A plant called pixie dust is supposed to grow there. If I give it to the elf king, he'll tell me what my father was doing the last time he was in town. Before he got arrested. Unless you know?"

He shook his head. "I didn't live here then. But I can come with you."

My heart skittered. "I lied to you," I said.

"You did," he confirmed. "But I misled you, too, numerous times, and honestly, I'm not sure I wouldn't have done the same in your position."

"I'm pretty sure you wouldn't have thrown glitter over Blythe's mother."

He grinned a little. "Okay, maybe not that part."

"Or wrestled Alissa off a broomstick while wearing a pair of Seven Millimetre Boots."

"You still have those? Even with the wings?"

Right… I still looked like a fairy. I'd honestly forgotten I hadn't re-glamoured. "Yeah. Do you mind?"

"Mind?" he echoed. "No. I told you, I don't care that you're a fairy. Or a witch. You're still Blair."

I could have kissed him on the spot, but I held off. And I grinned as he slipped his hand into mine to walk the rest of the way to the falls. He liked me as me. The stares would stop eventually. More importantly, I had my best friend back, Nathan and I might be able to make a go of it after all, and the town wasn't going to be overrun by hunters or collapse into confusion and unrest.

Now all I needed to do was deliver what the elf king needed.

From now on, I wouldn't be a witch in disguise, but fairy and witch both, and I wouldn't be afraid.

ABOUT THE AUTHOR

Elle Adams lives in the middle of England, where she spends most of her time reading an ever-growing mountain of books, planning her next adventure, or writing. Elle's books are humorous mysteries with a paranormal twist, packed with magical mayhem.

She also writes urban and contemporary fantasy novels as Emma L. Adams.

Find Elle on Facebook at https://www.facebook.com/pg/ElleAdamsAuthor/

9 781915 250186